THE
LONG-LOST TROLL

a Beatrice Sterling novel
by Barry Scott Will

ISBN (Paperback) 978-1-940919-06-5

Published in the United States of America by
Valutivity Press - www.valutivitypress.com

Illustrations by Ashton Leigh Will. Illustrations
copyright ©2017 by Valutivity LLC.

World of Berrea map by and ©2017 Valutivity LLC.

To Xander, who inspired the whole thing by playing "What if fantasy characters went to space in ships powered by magic?"

- Barry Scott Will

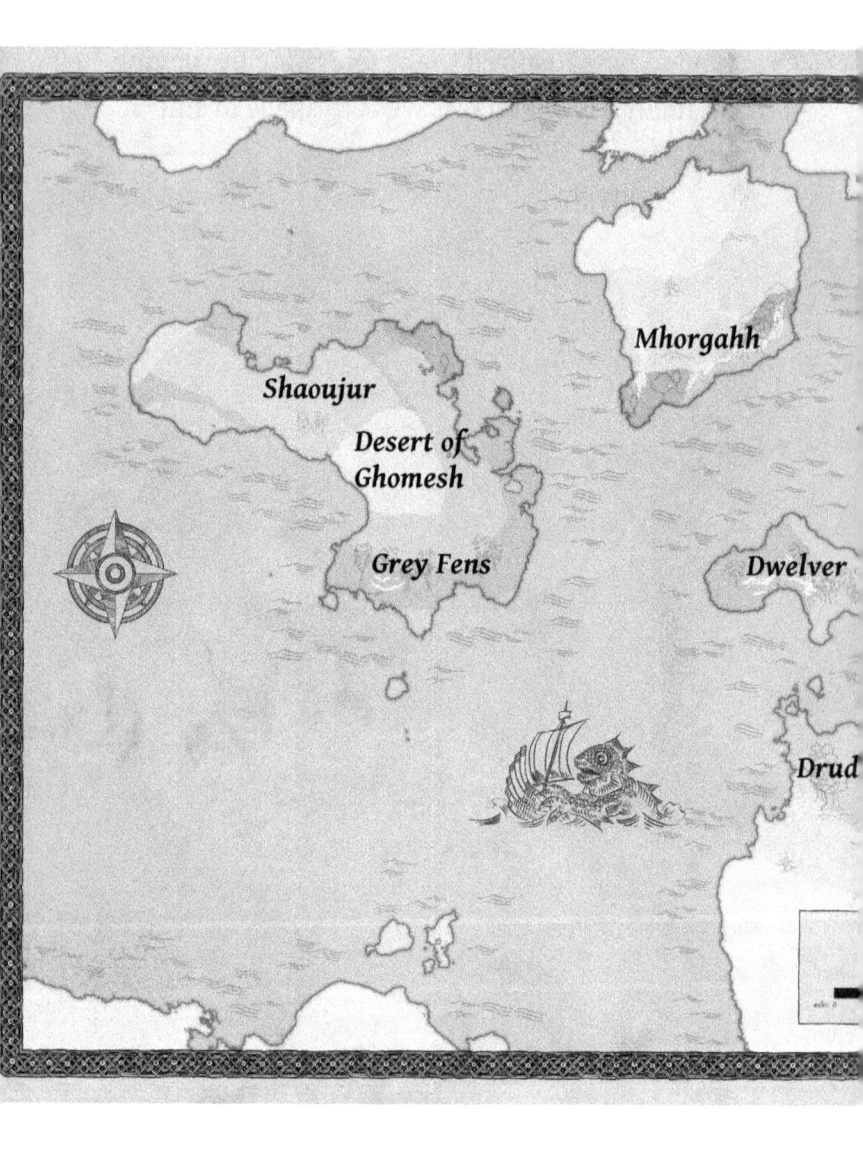

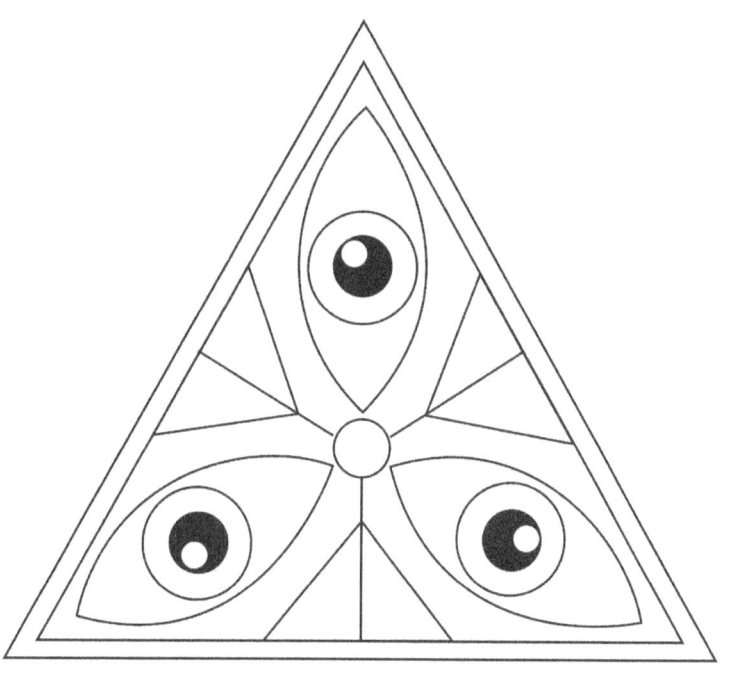

ONE

The distance before me was only a few steps, yet looked like leagues. Where I stood was Fisk, a cosmopolitan mélange of races brought together in common pursuit of wealth and power. Before me stood The Caverns—the troll slums of Fisk.

Trolls built their houses with interconnected upper stories and recessed ground floors leaving the streets as tunnels. Through the tunnel in front of me slouched several trolls—dirt and sweat matting the hair on their bodies, their clothes covered in grime, and gnarled beards covering their faces so all you could see were their eyes. Those eyes glared at me as they passed into Fisk proper, wondering what an outsider could want in their little corner of the city.

I had never entered The Caverns—had never *wanted* to enter The Caverns—but my current job required it. Mr. Cristof had sent me out to shut down a potion-making ring, and almost a month of investigating had led me here. I pulled out the piece of paper on which I had written directions to a shop and memorized them. I didn't want to act like I was lost or ask for help once I crossed into the slums.

Pocketing the paper, I took a deep breath and strode forward with feigned confidence. The sun disappeared and the air felt as though it were closing in around me. I hadn't gone more than a block when a troll leaning in a doorway stepped out in front of me.

"Where you going, skel?" He growled at me.

"That way," I responded in kind, pointing past him.

We glared at each other. I steeled my eyes and left my hands loose at my side. I didn't want to provoke him by reaching inside my jacket for a wand. He was the first to flinch. He slunk back into the doorway without saying anything, but his eyes never left me. I deliberately turned my back on him and continued on my way.

Signs above the doors advertised businesses, but in troll, which I couldn't understand. There were no windows looking out onto the streets, just blank stone walls, interrupted by recessed doors. It really felt like walking underground. My mind flashed back to the trek through the abandoned gold mine down in Darfa months ago, and I wondered what had become of Lilah. After a few tells, she had stopped calling and messages went unanswered. I couldn't get answers out of Mrs.

Kyle or Captain Brevery, either.

A passing troll bumped me harder than he needed to, and I wrenched my mind back to the task at hand. I stopped and got my bearings. I was supposed to go three blocks and turn right. Looking back, I figured I was in the third block and set off to the next cross street and turned right. I started looking at signs until I saw one with the word "Alkym" on it. That was my target.

I pushed open the door and walked into a dingy room lit with an actual candle lantern rather than one with a light ball inside. The room was empty except for a short counter. A troll leaning on the counter stared at me. He had dark hair and wore a vest with a symbol I knew—three eyes arranged inside an inverted triangle. It was the mark of the Treoynn, the potion-runners I was after.

The troll said nothing, so I smiled at him. "I'm looking for some potions," I said.

"Don't you have potion-makers where you live?" he snarled.

"Yeah, but I heard the most powerful potions are made here. I was told to come to your shop specifically."

He grunted. "I don't know who told you that, but if I find out, I might kill him for sending you here. Go away." He turned away.

"C'mon. Give a guy a hand, I really need some of the good stuff."

He whirled around and started to roar at me, "Go awa..." He choked off because I had a wand at his throat.

I leaned in close and stared directly into his widening eyes. "Listen to me and listen good. Two months ago, a woman threw herself off the top of the tallest tower in Fisk. She thought she could fly. And she did, but not for long, and then she fell—a long, long way down. A few days later, an ogre decided to have some fun by spitting fire from his fingers, then he started breathing fire, then he burned to ash from the inside out. A month ago, a guy walked into a tavern and tried to impress a girl by drinking an enlargement potion. They're still cleaning bits of him off the walls and ceilings. The girl's getting mental treatment from a 'path.

"Now, you and I know some people think potions are just harmless fun. And maybe the kind that get sold in Fisk proper *are* just that. They give you some nice dreams, let you levitate feathers, maybe light a candle by blowing on it. But somebody's selling stuff that's a lot more powerful. Too powerful. I've spent a month tracking them down and here I am. And I just want to know one thing."

The troll's eyes had narrowed during my speech. I

could see him staring at my wand and I knew what was coming next. There was just the faintest blink as the plan that had been rolling around in his brain went into action. He suddenly threw himself to the side while dropping down, where he probably had wands ready below the counter. Only, he never made it down there. At least, not in good shape.

At the first flinch of the muscles in his shoulder, I folded my arm and slammed my elbow into the side of his face. He went down and I vaulted over the counter and landed on top of him. This time, I put the tip of my wand right under one eye. He almost went cross-eyed trying to see it.

"Now, like I said, I just want to know one thing." I kept my voice even, punching each word individually. "Where. Are. You. Getting. Your. Potions?"

His voice trembled as he spoke, but he still had some nerve left in him. "I don't know where it comes from, and, even if I did, I wouldn't tell a skel."

"You think I'm going to believe you don't know where your own supply comes from?" I pressed the tip of the wand into his cheek right below the eye.

"A runner brings me potions. I don't know who makes them."

"Who's the runner?"

He didn't answer, just glared at me. His trembling was subsiding and I realized I wasn't going to get anywhere with him. I put a hand on his chest and pushed off, standing up with my wand still pointed directly at him. "Thanks for the help. You won't be seeing me again." I backed toward the door as he pulled himself up behind the counter.

I quickly backed to the door, pulled it in, and stepped out, pocketing my wand. I decided to vacate the area of the shop and walked quickly to the nearest intersection. I leaned against a wall and considered my options.

The shopkeeper was involved; the badge on his vest made that clear. And now the entire ring would know me and know I was onto them. I growled in frustration. I wanted to punch something, but the only productive punching would be to that shopkeeper's face, and that would be too dangerous now. I was going to have to find another place to dig.

I pushed myself away from the wall and right into a troll walking past. I had been so lost in thought, I was oblivious to what was going on around me. We both stumbled and I put my hands out to steady her. Like most troll women, she wore a hooded cape, trying to pass for human. She looked up from under the hood, gasped, and quickly turned and walked swiftly deeper into The Caverns.

My brain was racing, but I found myself following her before my thoughts could settle. She was hurrying along with her head down, pulling her cloak as far around herself as she could. I lengthened my stride to close on her. She turned down cross streets a couple of times and when she finally ducked into a doorway, I was only a few paces behind her.

I shoved open the door and stared at an empty room. Bare wooden walls framed a tiny room no more than a couple lengths on each side. There were no doors other than the one I had just come through and no sign of the troll. The only light came from a lantern hung on the wall next to the door.

I closed the door behind me and carefully ran my hands over the walls. I felt nothing, no faint outline of a hidden door, no concealed latches. Nothing. I sighed and let my head fall back as I leaned against a wall and there it was. The ceiling had a clearly defined trapdoor, but how did she get up through there so fast? And how was I supposed to get up there?

I looked back at the wall framing the door outside. I hadn't examined it before because I was looking for a way in, not a way out. Now I was looking for a way up. I reached out and grasped the lantern and it pulled away from the wall. With a thud, the trapdoor fell open and the upper side had ladder rungs carved into it.

I pulled myself up the door and had my second big shock. The room above me was spacious, light, and airy. Where the streets and lower floors were dank and dark, the walls of this room had many windows opening onto some type of courtyard. Sunlight streamed into the room, illuminating rustic furniture, paintings hung on the walls, and two trolls—a man and a woman—sitting on a divan, staring at me.

I reached down and hauled the trapdoor closed and walked over to the couple and stood there in silence for a moment, staring at the face of the woman I had chased through the streets. Her big, golden eyes were wide and her mouth was turned down in a bigger frown than usual.

"Hello, Lilah."

TWO

The male troll rose up and started to growl at me, "You're not wanted here..." He turned as Lilah laid a hand on his arm.

"It's OK, Alinn. Leave us for a moment." He stared at her, then turned to regard me with a hostile stare. Baring his teeth at me, he stalked from the room.

"What are you doing here, Betty?"

"May I sit?" I asked by way of answering.

"I'd rather you didn't."

I sat down beside her anyway. She slid to the far end of the divan. I settled in, putting an arm along the back cushions. I was trying to be casual.

"So...What have you been up to?"

"Why are you here, Betty?" She was harshly demanding.

"I followed you. I was curious why you were trying to hide yourself in The Caverns, and why you didn't acknowledge me when we bumped into each other."

She stood suddenly and walked over to the windows looking out over the courtyard. She stood in silence for several moments. I decided not to push her. When she turned back, she had softened.

"I'm sorry, Betty. I know you've been trying to reach me, but I didn't want you to get caught up in my problems."

"What happened in Darfa?" I asked. "When I left, things were looking up."

"That didn't last long," she laughed bitterly. "Harris charged me with an illegal, hostile takeover of his Hold. I was brought up before the Directors' Court and found guilty. My Hold was stripped from me and given to Harris, and I was exiled. I didn't know where to go, so I..."

"You could have called me!" I exploded out of my seat. "I would have come right away! We would have given Harris more of what we gave him before. They can't..."

Lilah stopped me by putting her hands on my chest. "That's exactly why I didn't call you, Betty. I knew you would want to solve the problem that way, but...that would have only made it worse. I had the best legal team I could find working on my case and they're still appealing the decision, but..." She sighed. "I don't think it's going to help. When you get down to it, we did attack Harris's seaport, which was in unclaimed territory."

"After he attacked us! Or did you forget those constructs?"

"No, I didn't forget," she snapped. "But..." Her shoulders sagged. "We were in his territory. Uninvited." She turned away again. "It's a lost cause, Betty. I've got to start over. Alinn is a distant cousin, so I came here to stay for a while until I decide what to do."

For some reason the fact the other troll was a relative made me feel relieved. I tried to tamp that down. "Are you sure you don't want to go back and fight Harris? We beat him once."

"No, Betty. The lawyers and courts are working on it, but I'm out of it unless I have to return for testimony. Which doesn't seem likely; my lawyers tell me they can't get a judge to even sit for the appeal."

"Well, if you're serious about starting over, you should get out of Fisk. There isn't much here for trolls, especially women. Unless you want to be a washer-woman or make cheap jewelry to sell at market."

She slowly walked back to the divan and sat down, burying her face in her hands. "I know," she whispered. "I've been here long enough to see how Durgahh are treated. And how we treat others." She looked up. "But *you* still haven't told me why you were in The Caverns."

"You're changing the subject."

"Yes, I am."

I sighed. "I'm looking into a potion scam. Some group is making overpowered potions and people are dying from them."

"And you think Durgahh are behind it?" There was an accusing note of scorn in her voice.

"I don't know *who* is making the potions. I've spent a month on this and finally found one of the distributors. And, yes, it was a shop here in The Caverns. I didn't get any answers from the merchant, and now the gang knows I'm onto them. They'll probably pack up and move and I'll have to start over again as well." I grinned sarcastically at her. "A time of new beginnings for us both!"

"Don't do that, Betty. You're not very good at it. Can I help you?"

"You want to help me? I thought you were the one needing help."

"Right now, the best thing is for me to find something to do. Is Joshua paying you enough to hire an assistant?"

"How do you know I'm working for Cristof?"

"Don't be silly. Once Joshua gets his hooks into you, you're trapped."

"Oh. I thought you were reading my mind."

"You're still wearing your hood. I can't hear you."

Her voice was flat. "And why should that bother you? You know I'm a telepath."

I cursed myself for panicking at the thought of Lilah reading my mind, and for revealing my panic to her. To soften the blow, I reached up and slid the gold-threaded mail coif off. The gold thread hid my thoughts from passing 'paths and I was so used to wearing it, I hardly ever took it off.

"By the way," I avoided her question, "why didn't you go to Cristof for help?"

"Now you're changing the subject."

I just widened my eyes innocently.

She sighed. "I did. He told me to wait, that something good was coming. But I'm tired of waiting. I'm tired of sitting around, crying over spilt milk. *Please*, let me work for you, Betty."

I already knew the answer, and, now that I had my hood off, so did she. "All right. I can afford ten marks a day, but only for a month or so. If the job takes longer than that, we'll have to re-negotiate." I was trying to be all business, but she threw that right out the window with a big grin and throwing her arms around me.

"Thank you, Betty," she said as she hugged me. "Where do we start?" She stepped back, but kept her hands on my arms.

"I...don't know." I disengaged myself and went to

stand by the windows. The courtyard outside was completely enclosed by buildings, but it was open to the sun and full of trees and bushes with stone paths meandering through. "This is really something. I had no idea the trolls were hiding these gardens."

Lilah came up beside me. "The Durgahh here in Fisk don't want others to disturb them, so they make the outside as uninviting as possible. To keep their own spirits from being as dark as their streets, they build everything around gardens filled with plants from Durgahh. It gives them a little piece of home." She looked up at me. "But you're not answering my question. What's next?"

At that moment, her cousin, Alinn, came back into the room. "Is the skel finished here, Lilahh?"

"No, Alinn, he's going to be staying for a little while. Could you get us some tea?" She smiled sweetly at him. He gave her a startled look, then glared at me again before slouching back out of the room.

Lilah moved back over to the divan and I followed. "He said your name a little differently, didn't he?" I asked.

"Yes," she replied. "He used the proper Durgahh pronunciation of my name. Lilahh."

"Lilah?"

"No, you're not saying it right. It's 'Lilahh.'"

"I don't get it."

"Well, you're not Durgahh."

I decided to stop there. "OK," I said as I sat down beside her. This time she didn't slide away. "Like I said, I tracked down a distributor here in The Caverns, but he wouldn't talk, and now I'm afraid the gang is on to me. However, I do have a name and symbol to work with. They call themselves Treoynn and they identify themselves with a patch that looks like a triangle with three eyes inside it."

Lilah gasped. "Can I see the symbol?"

"Sure." I concentrated on the image of the patch I had seen on the shopkeeper. Lilah focused on me for a moment, then sank back and sighed.

"I know who they are," she said, matter-of-factly.

"What? How? Who are they? Where can we find them?" The questions came pouring out.

"Slow down, Betty," she said. She stood and extended her hand, "Come with me."

I followed her out of the room, down a short hall, and into a small bedroom. It was sparse and undecorated, with only a bed and a small bureau. I guessed she hadn't been here long enough to make it her own. Lilah opened the top drawer of the bureau and rummaged around until she found a small, metal cube.

"Here," she said, handing me the cube, "take a look at these."

I placed the cube against my forehead and concentrated on it. Images began flickering in my mind, scenes of a troll family—man, woman, and child. The child looked familiar and I realized I was looking at scenes from Lilah's childhood and these must be her parents. Then I noticed the vests worn by both adults—they had the Treoynn patch on them. I hastily pulled the memory cube away and stared at Lilah.

"Treoynn is my clan name. My mother's clan was Burkahh, and I took that name when we left Durgaland. The symbol is our clan's totem. I don't know if the whole clan is involved in your potion gang, or just some of them, but they are announcing loud and clear who they are. Any Durgahh would know exactly who they are dealing with."

"So this is big..." I began, and Lilah nodded. I tried to formulate my thoughts. "We could hunt around here for who knows how long, or we could go to Durgaland and find the source."

"We don't know they're coming from Durgaland," Lilah protested. "They could still be local, just trading on the clan's name."

"Would any troll announce a clan affiliation if they weren't being supported by the clan?"

"No," she whispered. "They would be fools to drag the Treoynn name into this if the clan chief weren't involved. Otherwise, as soon as he found out, he'd have them all hunted down and killed."

"So we have to go to Durgaland."

"I can't. Especially not back to my clan's demesne."

"Your clan's what?"

"Demesne. The lands owned and worked by the Treoynn. Each Durgahh clan has its own lands they farm and hunt and broaching another clan's demesne is considered an act of war."

"But why can't you go back? Does it have something to do with your parents?"

She paused, and then sat on the bed. I leaned up against the doorframe.

"As you know," she began, "I'm a very powerful telepath. My ability manifested early, but my parents tried to hide it. I think they suspected what would happen when the clan chief found out. Of course, he did find out. I was twelve. My parents came into my room in the middle of the night and told me the chief was going to take me and force me to use my talent on prisoners—especially prisoners of war. We were going to run.

"I grabbed a few things, whatever I could fit into a single pack, and we set off, on foot, through the night. My parents had dragon-hide caps, one for each of us, so we would be hidden from any telepathic searchers. We snuck out of town and set off for my mother's clan demesne. We figured we could hide there, but we were wrong. We reached the Burkahh lands easily enough, and asked for help from my mother's cousins. They allowed us to stay, but went to the Burkahh chief and he refused to allow us to stay with their clan. He didn't want to start a clan war with the Treoynn.

"So, we had to run again. We decided to leave Durgaland and come to Fisk. Father had relatives here," she gestured outward, "Alinn's parents, and we figured they wouldn't care if we were wanted people. But, on the way to the nearest port, a dragon found us..."

Her voice trailed off and tears began pooling in her eyes. "Have you ever seen a dragon?" I shook my head. "They're huge and they don't normally come down out of the mountains. I don't know why this one was so close to the sea, but he came charging into our camp just after daybreak. We had no weapons other than my parents' wands, and those are useless against a dragon."

She paused, her head down and shoulders trembling. I thought about going and sitting beside her, but decided that would be too much and just stood, watching in silence. She finally pulled herself together. "Father screamed at mother and me to run and used his wand to distract the dragon. Mother grabbed me and ran. We ran until we couldn't any longer, hearing the roars of the dragon the whole time. We collapsed in a thicket and mother dragged me under the branches and we lay there, heaving. We could hear the dragon's roars getting further away and then they died out completely and we just lay there. I was crying, and I think that was the only thing that kept mother from losing it herself.

"She finally dragged me out, shook me a little and told me we had to get moving. We couldn't let father's sacrifice be in vain. We made it to Banjall and tried to find a ship coming to Fisk." She paused again, collecting her thoughts. "There were Treoynn waiting for us on the docks. I don't know how they found us, maybe they were just watching all the major ports. Mother pulled out her wand and told me to run..."

Lilah began sobbing in earnest. This time I sat down and put my arm around her, but said nothing. "Both my parents sacrificed themselves for me," she choked out. Taking a deep breath, she continued, "I jumped into the harbor and swam under the docks. I kept swimming until I saw a ship casting off, then I swam to it and grabbed a trailing rope. When they finally pulled it up, they had me and were already far enough out in the harbor to not want to turn around. So they let me stay on board until they reached their first stop, which was Braysport. I eventually ended up in Darfa and worked my way up..."

She paused for a long time. "Anyway, you know

how that ended. I can't go back to Durgaland. I just can't."

I sat holding her, not wanting to break the silence just yet. Then I had a thought. "Why don't we go get that tea your cousin was making for us?"

"Do you drink tea?"

"Not really, but I thought it would help."

"Well, we'll have to make it ourselves. Alinn would never serve anything to a non-Durgahh. I just told him that to make him go away."

I chuckled. She smiled. Then we both started laughing. The release of tension and emotion helped both of us calm down. We returned to the main room and sat together on the divan. For a while, neither of us spoke.

"You really do need to go to the Treoynn in Durgahh," Lilah said. "You'll probably need a guide. Someone who's familiar with the country, the customs, and the language." I nodded in agreement. She looked at me with a little smile. "Do you still have those nausea bracelets I made for you?"

I nodded again. "Are you ready for me to book passage to Durgaland?" I asked.

She stared at me for a while, but her eyes were focused inward. "Yes," she stated. "It's time for me to go home."

THREE

Lilah and I stood at the prow of *Kroschk* as the cargo ship maneuvered into the port of Banjall. The ogres running the ship had been happy to make a few extra marks renting out one of their storerooms to a couple of small people, as long as we provided our own food, and bedding. We had spent two days camped out in a "closet" that was bigger than my apartment back in Fisk. The air was brisk and the wind ruffled our coats and the fine hairs on Lilah's hands and face.

She caught me looking at her and smiled. Patting my hand, she turned to go. "Let's pack our things. We'll be docking soon, and I want to get away from the smell of ogre food as quickly as possible."

An hour later we docked, thanked the captain, and hurried ashore into Banjall. "Let me do the talking," Lilah whispered. "Some of these Durgahh might speak Menskel, but better to just let me handle all communication."

"Speak what?"

"Menskel. Human. The Durgahh name for your people."

"Is that why some trolls call me a skel?"

"Yes, but you're getting off track. Pay attention. Some Durgahh are likely to try and trick you by pretending not to understand everything you say. Don't say anything to me you don't want public unless you're sure we're alone."

"I'll follow your lead."

Banjall looked a lot like other seaports with large warehouses fronting the docks and commercial buildings beyond them providing everything a seaman with shore leave could want. And then some. Lilah led me through the commercial center, into residential areas beyond. She was searching for something and finally led me to a small house in the middle of dozens of other houses that all looked the same.

She rapped on the door, then spoke with a person on the other side. After a moment, the door opened and a tall troll woman peeked out. She and Lilah spoke some more, of which the only word I recognized was Lilah's name. Eventually she hugged Lilah and stepped back from the door so we could enter.

"These are friends of Alinn. He sent word that his cousin would be coming and asked them to help us for a day or so while we're here. I thought this would be better than registering at an inn."

None of Alinn's friends spoke human, so I was left out of the loop on all the conversation Lilah had with them. But they fed us well, and the bed was comfortable. At least, Lilah told me it was comfortable, since I slept on the floor as they only had the one bed for guests. In the morning, Lilah pulled a Treoynn vest out of her bag.

"I had Alinn track one down before we left," she answered my raised eyebrow. "I figured the easiest way to get into the Treoynn demesne is to act like I'm coming home."

"You're really buying into this now," I said.

"If they're running potions into other lands, then bringing them down will be the best way to repay them for my parents."

"Two-birds-with-one-stone deal. But, there's only the one vest. What about me?"

"A non-Durgahh caught wearing a Durgahh clan vest would be killed immediately."

"I probably shouldn't wear one, then."

"You'll be my bodyguard. It's a common thing for Durgahh who have been traveling abroad to hire locals to defend them."

"OK, so where are we going?"

"We'll go to the Burkahh demesne first. It's only two or three days travel from here on foot and I should still be welcome there, if I can find my mother's relatives. We can learn more about what's happening in the Treoynn demesne, since they border one another. And then..."

"And then we plan our attack," I finished her thought.

"Yes, something like that," she smiled.

We had brought camping supplies with us, so packing was just a matter of begging some food from our hosts. We set off through the city streets, heading north.

"I don't see a lot of floaters," I commented. "Or even any wagons, or horses. Just lots of trolls carrying bags or pulling small carts."

Lilah didn't immediately answer my question, just looked nervously around for a moment. "You need to start calling us Durgahh. I've gotten used to the other word from years living in the Southlands, but here...You need to forget the t-word."

"I'll try, but...really? It's not a term of disrespect, it's just what your people are called."

"Maybe you don't *mean* disrespect, but Durgahh are proud and only want to be known by our name for ourselves."

"And when they call me 'skel?'"

"This is our land. You'll have to take it, just like I had to take 'troll.'" She whispered the last word lest any passing trolls—I mean, Durgahh—might hear.

"OK. But you still haven't answered my question. Why so few vehicles and animals?"

"Mostly because of dragons."

"Are they really that bad? And why would they keep you from using floaters?"

"Yes, they really are that bad. They live up in the mountains, but don't come down into the forests very often because they don't like crawling through the trees."

"Why don't they fly in?"

"Dragons can't fly," she snorted.

"But, all the stories..."

"That's what they are. Stories. They're way too big and don't even have wings. Occasionally," she continued her previous explanation, "one gets hungry enough or angry enough to come into the forests and then you've got to either kill it or chase it back into the mountains—neither of which is easy and usually results in the death of Durgahh hunters."

She paused and I remembered her father died at the teeth of a dragon who had invaded the forest. "Anyway," she continued, "we don't build wide roads for floaters or other vehicles because that would make it easier for the dragons to get to our villages. We don't keep or raise many animals because it would encourage dragons to come after easy prey."

She looked around at the buildings. "We live under constant threat of the dragons. If they weren't so slow to breed and so aggressive that they kill each other, we couldn't exist here. No one could." She shook herself. "A few large cities exist on the coastline because the dragons won't get near the sea, but the rest of the Durgahh live in small clans in walled villages in the middle of the forests. We farm and raise animals only inside the walls. Mostly we hunt and gather wild vegetables and fruit. Outside this city...it will be like stepping back into another age."

"Why do so many tr—Durgahh stay?"

"We're Durgahh. This is our home." She lapsed into a brooding silence and didn't speak again until we had passed the northern gates and entered the forest. The road leading out of Banjall quickly narrowed into a footpath as it entered the tree line and we soon found ourselves alone among the trees.

"Why so many switchbacks in the path? We're not going uphill."

"Dra..."

"Dragons," I interrupted. "Yeah, I get it. Your people sure live in fear of dragons."

"If you ever meet one," she answered softly, "you will understand. Pray that you don't."

"So, if the dragons are so bad, and it's so hard to move things, where do all the potions come from?"

"Do you know how potions are made?"

"Not really, no. Never had a reason to ask."

"Potions are alchemical. A spell is melded to a chunk of metallic mineral, then the mineral is ground up and mixed in the right amounts in different types of potable liquids. When a person drinks the potion, the spell infused in it gives that person the same talent for a brief time. Durgahh are really good at the alchemy—mixing the minerals and the liquids."

Lilah sighed heavily. "Durgahh are also really cheap labor. Durgahh villages are not swimming in tech and life in this environment is hard. The clans cut deals with the corps. The clans supply the alchemical labor by sending clan members to the cities to work in the potion factories. The corps pay the living expenses for the workers and pay the clans directly for the labor, sometimes in marks, but mostly in tech. Working conditions aren't great and a lot of Durgahh escape across the Straights and try to live among the Menskel."

"Where do all the minerals come from? I don't see any evidence of mining."

"The ore is shipped over the Straights by the corps. It's cheaper for them to do that than to pay the high prices for elves in Ilanerra, and humans and ogres aren't very good at alchemy. Sometimes the ore is already melded, but mostly not. Trollmen—what we call our techs—come from the villages to the cities to meld spells. My father was a talented tech—trollmen—and he would be away for a month or so at a time."

"It all seems unnecessarily complicated."

"Corps will go to a great deal of complication to save money."

We reached the Burkahh demesne around the middle of the third day. We could probably have shaved some time off the trip had we cut straight through the woods, but Lilah insisted on sticking to the path, which meandered aimlessly, often reversing direction in some mad scheme to make it more impassable to dragons. I didn't complain, though; the trip gave Lilah and me a lot of time to talk. Back in her homeland at last, she opened up, and we chatted about everything from favorite vacation spots to the best way to leverage capital assets to achieve a buyout on credit rather than with cash.

Actually, Lilah did most of the talking on the latter subject. Once I displayed a sympathetic ear for details about hold management, she talked endlessly of the details of her old job. I didn't understand most of what she was saying, but figured it was better conversation than me talking about my old job. The details of being an enforcer for the corps don't make for friendly conversation.

The main village of the Burkahh demesne was surrounded by a log palisade approximately as tall as an ogre and covering an area equal to several city blocks. Durgahh guards standing at the gate watched as we approached and one took off running into the village when we were several lengths away. The other guard merely nodded at us as we walked through the open gate.

"Why the gate and guards if they just let people walk in?" I whispered to Lilah.

"The gate is for keeping out dragons, not people, and the guards are for closing the gate if they see or hear a dragon approaching. It does get closed at night, though."

The Durgahh in the village stopped and stared at us—or, I should say, me—as we walked by. Lilah pulled out a piece of paper with hastily scrawled writing and a crude diagram and stopped to look at it.

"The house we're looking for is over toward the north side of the village," she said. She set off through the houses.

There were no streets, as such, in the village. Rather, it was more a collection of small farms. Each home had its own extensive vegetable gardens surrounding it and usually a small barn or other animal shelter. Paths meandered, sometimes seeming to run right through someone's property. The houses were all two or more stories tall and had overhanging upper stories, but with the amount of separation between each, there were none of the cavernous passageways found in the slums of Fisk.

"Why the overhanging upper stories?" I queried Lilah.

She replied while still examining the directions on the paper and looking around. "It gives us more living space while maximizing arable ground around the houses."

I looked closer and saw the gardens did run right up to the walls of each house.

"All this is because of dragons, right?" She nodded while still trying to follow her sheet of directions. "Well then," I continued, "what about the wooden walls? If dragons are this big of an issue, how come everything's made of wood—even the wall around the village?"

She finally stopped and stared at me. "What has that got to do with anything?"

"If a dragon attacked this place it would just burn it down. You should use stone or something less flammable."

She snorted, "Dragons don't breathe fire."

"But the..." I started, as she continued on her way.

"Yes, the stories," she interrupted. "And do you also believe an intelligent fairy collects the teeth of children from under their head as they sleep?"

"Well, no, but..."

"Look," she said, stopping again and turning to me. "Dragons are not huge, flying lizards raining fire and destruction from the sky. They're big and they do look like giant lizards, but they're covered with fur—usually white. They are completely immune to tech, which is why it's so hard to fight them. Spells just bounce off their hide, which is also very resistant to sharp, pointy things. They don't breathe fire, but their teeth and claws will rip you to shreds in a few breaths, and their tail can take out a tree if they get enough swinging space. They may not be like the stories, but they're bad enough. Now, if you have no more questions about the local fauna, I think this is the place."

Lilah had stopped at a homestead built up against the wall of the village. She began picking her way through rows of some type of bean plant, but stopped as the door opened and a male troll Durgahh stepped out and pulled the door closed behind him. They spoke briefly and his eyes widened. He went back inside and Lilah stood still, waiting. I suppressed the urge to ask what was going on.

After a short time, the door opened again and a wizened Durgahh gingerly walked out of the house, supported by the man who had come out earlier. She peered at Lilah as they approached, drinking in her face. At last she stood before Lilah and reached out to touch her face, then broke into tears and grabbed Lilah, who had also begun crying and hugged the old woman back.

Lilah finally turned and looked at me, "This is my mother's mother. She thought we were all dead." Lilah turned back around and took her grandmother's arm and they walked toward the house.

FOUR

Not long after we arrived, a knock at the door announced an emissary of the Burkahh chief wanting to know what a Treoynn Durgahh was doing in their village. I caught the work "skel" frequently, so I tried to look innocent and unassuming—not easy when you're the biggest person in the room. I had spent so much of my life around ogres, who are twice my size, I had forgotten how tall and broad I was, especially compared to trolls. After he left, Lilahh told me they convinced the official she was just a relative and he let it go.

Once the official was out the door, still glaring at me as he left, Lilah outlined our next steps.

"In a Durgahh clan," she told me, "everyone knows everyone else. We can't just walk in and blend in. I might be seen as a stranger wearing the clan symbol, which is a crime. So, instead, I want to be recognized as the little girl whose family ran away twenty years ago. I should be welcomed home and, because I'm gifted, we could find ourselves in the inner circle of the clan chief. To make sure that happens, I will send a cousin with a message to the chief."

"I heard 'should' and 'could' in there. What are you not telling me?"

"Well, like I told you before, the chief wanted to exploit my telepathy, which my parents thought would be harmful for a young girl, so they ran away with me. According to my grandmother, that chief died several years ago and his grandson took over. He would be a little younger than I am and probably isn't holding a grudge, if he even remembers my family."

"But he might be resentful, and we would walk into the village and immediately be thrown into jail."

"That's why I sent a message to him. If he's still angry about something that happened when he was a little boy, my cousin will warn me and we can figure out a different plan."

"Did you consider," I said carefully, "that the chief might act like he's happy you're back, just to get us to walk into town so he can punish you?"

"Um, I was sort of hoping that wouldn't be one of the options."

"Well, at least you thought about it," I sighed.

It took four days for Lilahh's cousin to travel to the Treoynn village and return. I hated waiting, but had no other choice. To pass the time, I pried more information about Durgahh culture out of Lilahh.

Durgahh were very clan-oriented, with each clan being more an extended family than a disparate collection of individuals. Multiple generations of the same family lived and worked together. The rustic villages and function of the clans was based partly on the harsh climate, partly on the threat of the dragons, and partly from the lack of technicians. Tech ability was rare among Durgahh, which was the primary reason Lilah was sure we—or, at least, she—would be welcomed back to her old clan. Most Durgahh clans depended on the potion trade with the "Southlands," as they called Ilannera, especially for getting what tech they had.

Durgahh still largely did a lot of things the "old-fashioned" way, though I had noticed a fair amount of tech in the homes. Lilah told me when Durgahh traded with Ilannera, they focused on personal items like cookpads or water pumps. The constant threat of dragons kept Durgahh clans from wanting to clear vast amounts of forest for farming or building large cities, and this was the primary reason young trolls often went to work in the seaports or left Durgaland altogether. Despite the treatment trolls usually received, the big cities of Ilanerra offered plentiful tech for living a "more comfortable" life, as Lilah put it. Reflecting on The Caverns, I wasn't so sure it was an improvement for those trolls—notwithstanding the courtyard garden views.

When Lilah's cousin returned, he brought word the current Treoynn chief would be happy to welcome back a long-lost member of the clan. It was at this point Lilah's grandmother threw a fit. I had to wait to learn the gist of the shouting match, but she essentially had no intention of letting her granddaughter out of her sight now that Lilah was "back from the dead." There was much yelling and a great deal of crying and Lilah wouldn't even talk about it until we had left the village. However, by the next morning, the grandmother had calmed down enough to hug and kiss Lilah goodbye. She even hugged me and said something to me, which Lilah loosely translated as, "Bring my granddaughter back, or I'll hunt you down myself."

I smiled at the old Durgahh while assessing she probably could do just that.

We reached Treoynn sometime after midday of the second day of our journey. We were immediately whisked to the chief's home, which, while larger than other houses in the village, would never qualify as a "palace," and given rooms.

Once freshened up from our journey, we were thrown a party by the villagers, outdoors around large fire pits that were roasting some kind of meat, generating a mouthwatering aroma. Lilah told me it was dragon meat and laughed at my surprised expression.

"Yes, they are dangerous," she said, "but they're killable. When a dragon does come down from the mountains, hunting parties will try to drive it back, but they have developed a few strategies for trapping them and killing them. A full-grown dragon can feed a village for a month and their hide is used for the leather shirts the hunters wear."

I had noticed the leather aprons many of the male trolls wore, but had not asked about them. The shirts draped to their knees, much like my chain shirt and were mostly a pale brown or whitish color. "They're very tough," Lilah continued, "and they're completely spell-resistant, just as when the dragon was living." I made a mental note not to get into a tech fight with a troll; it wouldn't do either of us any good, considering how we were armored.

For me, the night dragged on. None of the trolls could speak human—or didn't admit they could. While Lilah spent far more time talking than eating, I mostly sat in the background constantly nibbling at this or that plate of food.

Later, Lilah told me nothing of any consequence was said—which was frustrating, because there were no doubt many things I could have picked up about her, her childhood, her family if I had only understood their language. The conversation had apparently spun around villagers expressing gratitude for her return, since most of them knew her family. Apparently, the Treoynn clan believed her family had been killed while on a trip to visit the Burkahh clan and were unaware of the circumstances forcing her parents to flee.

When I finally slouched into my room to sleep, I had "nibbled" way too much and was afraid overeating would keep me up all night. But the luxury of having my own bed—albeit a length too short--and not having to sleep on the floor, allowed me a peaceful slumber. Unfortunately, it wasn't very long, as I was beckoned out of bed by a male troll who wordlessly motioned me to follow him.

Outside, the sun was barely showing above the trees and the village was enveloped in the gray wash of early dawn. A large group of trolls wearing their leather armor and carrying a variety of weapons was gathered around the remains of the pit fire from the previous night. The trolls were whispering among themselves, but no one seemed to be taking any action until Lilah came out, with her sleeping blanket wrapped around herself to ward off the morning chill.

One of the trolls then began speaking loudly as everyone else quieted down. At one point, he pointed toward me and one of the trolls beside me clapped me on the back and grinned at me. I looked over at Lilah and saw shock and fear on her face as she stared at the speaker. The speech didn't last long, and then the armed trolls began moving toward the village gate. I looked at Lilah and shrugged to indicate my confusion. She just stared at me for a moment while trying to find her voice.

"A dragon has been spotted nearby," she whispered. "They're going after it and want you to come along."

"Oh, well, after you've talked them up so much, I'd kind of like to see one." I turned to go get my gear.

"No!" Lilah jumped and grabbed my arm. "I forbid it!"

"You...Never mind. Look, we need to gain their trust. There are a lot of them and they know what they're doing. Relax, I'll get a good look at a real dragon, and maybe I'll get some of its hide for armor." I grinned at her, shook off her hand and trotted back to my room. Once armed and armored, I hurried toward the gate, where the trolls were gathered.

As I strode up to the group of hunters, one of the trolls stared at the wand bandolier across my chest, shook his head and handed me his longspear and looked a question at me. It had been years since I had trained with polearms, but I quickly fell into the rhythm as I executed a few basic forms with it. The troll smiled approvingly. The group moved out in two loose columns and headed into the woods. I fell in at the back. These were the folks with experience fighting dragons; I just wanted to watch.

We quickly turned into the woods and the trolls fanned out as they slipped through the undergrowth. I was really out of my element here and blundered noisily through the forest, earning me several disapproving stares. We had not gone far when the leader held up a hand to stop and everyone dropped into a squat. He signaled one troll, who melted into the forest. I became aware of a grunting rumble from deeper in the woods.

In a few moments, the scout returned and whispered to the commander, who motioned all of us to move out to our left. The trolls moved low and stealthily through the trees and I tried as best as I could to emulate them. I hoped the noise made by the dragon obscured the noise I made as I randomly stepped on twigs and scuffled leaves. The troll who had given me his spear just shook his head and put his finger to his lips, so I slowed down even more and was able to get rid of most of the noise I was making.

The group turned to the right and the trolls began compacting their spread formation. One troll stood up and raised a small flag and stared at it intently. It fluttered a bit toward our rear, which satisfied the leader and we crept forward. The dragon came into view in flashes as the trees thinned out toward a clearing. We were approaching it from its back quarter, so I could only get an oblique view of it.

I couldn't see the head as it was down to the ground obviously eating something, but the body looked something like a bear with a long, thick tail. It stood a little taller than me at the shoulder and at least five times that in length, of which maybe half was tail. Dirty, white fur covered the body and the rear legs were a bit larger than the forelegs. Its feet were buried in the matted leaves of the forest floor, but I imagined they would be suitably equipped with claws.

My companion troll motioned me off toward the left, around behind the dragon, and we crept carefully to the wing of the hunting group. The other trolls shifted slightly to the right. The troll with me pointed to the spear, then to the dragon, and then to his own stomach. I got the idea, the proper place to stick the weapon would be in the underbelly of the beast. I nodded and gripped the spear a little tighter. I looked toward the commander, who was looking up and down his line of hunters.

Satisfied we were ready, the commander stood up, motioning the rest of us to stand as well, pulled a wand from his belt and shot a fireball at the ground near the beast's head. The explosion startled the dragon, who reared back and roared. With its large hind legs and tail the beast could stand upright, completely exposing the soft underside. I leaped forward and thrust my spear toward the joint in the dragon's haunch, but I was too far to the side and the spear merely grazed the tougher hide of the beast's side.

I danced back toward the trees and that's when I realized the trolls were gone. I looked around as I backpedaled, but could see none of the trolls who had been ranged out beside me just moments before, and that's when the dragon's tail struck me and sent me flying into the forest.

The shock of impact stunned me a bit, but instinct caused me to twist and roll as I hit the ground. I scuttled behind a large tree and paused. The dragon was muttering, not roaring, and I risked a glance around the tree. It was still in the clearing, and was sniffing the air, weaving its head from side to side. We had approached downwind and I hoped that was still the case. I finally got a good look at its head, with an elongated snout and large, tufted ears that looked like horns. I imagined its hearing would be as good as, if not better than its sense of smell, so moving was not immediately possible.

I had lost my spear when the tail hit me, not that such a weapon would help in a one-on-one fight between me and the beast. Not knowing what else to do, I stayed behind my tree and kept watching the dragon. After not catching smell nor sound of anything, it returned to whatever had been occupying it when we arrived. I decided now was a good time to tiptoe away.

Not a good idea. Not at all.

The sound of rustling leaves brought the dragon's head around with a grunt and it launched itself into the trees toward me. I took off at an angle, trying to get the beast to twist itself around the trees. Getting behind another trunk, I pulled out my fire wand, ducked out to my left and fired an explosion into the ground right in front of the dragon's head.

The beast scrambled back from the explosion and I ran deeper into the forest. Having a sudden inspiration, I sheathed my fire wand and pulled out my nature wand. I could hear the crashing of the dragon behind me, so I threw myself behind a large tree and looked out. The dragon was several lengths behind me, struggling to shoulder its way past the trees. I stepped out, which caused the animal to charge toward me with renewed vigor. I calmly sliced the tree next to me and turned and ran as it crashed down.

The dragon roared and I risked a look over my shoulder. The tree I had cut had only fallen over a little and been caught in the branches of another tree, but, the dragon was partially trapped under the angled trunk and screaming as it tried to shove its way out. Its back feet were braced on either side of two trees and it was trying to scrabble backwards with its front claws.

I kept backing up, slowly, staring at the beast, trying to figure out where it might go or what it might do, and that's when I noticed the trees on either side of the dragon had grown bigger. I stopped and stared and, yes, the trees were growing. The dragon was frantic by now, thrashing about and screaming as the boles on either side grew closer together, squeezing tighter. Suddenly, with a loud crack of breaking bone, the dragon stiffened, then went limp as blood fountained from its mouth.

"You should have shot it in the mouth."

The voice startled me so much, I jumped backward, tripped over a branch and ended sprawled out on my back in the forest undergrowth. A troll walked from behind a tree nearby and ambled over to me. "You shoot them inside the mouth while they're roaring," he repeated. "Their insides aren't resistant like their hides."

"So, why didn't you..." I began.

"Do you see any wands on me?" He asked rhetorically. Indeed, his clothes were tattered and obviously old and well-worn, and he had no place to keep anything. "I'm a trollmen and working with plants is one of my skills," he gestured toward the dead dragon and the now huge trees that formed the vice that killed it. He stared at me intently, "I know my brothers aren't fond of skels, but what caused them to set you up as a dragon's meal?"

"Set me up? Your brothers? Wait, who are you?"

He sighed and shook his head, transferring his stare to the ground. He looked back up at me, "Let's get away from here. They're bound to come back to really drive the dragon off." He glanced over at the corpse, "At least they'll get a month's worth of meat and plenty of hide from that one."

He reached a hand out to me and helped me scramble up, then took off jogging through the forest. When I didn't follow, he turned back and asked, "Why aren't you coming?"

"I don't know you. I don't know what you want."

He barked a short laugh, "I'm the guy who just saved you from the death planned by your 'friends.' I'm your best bet at getting out of Durgaland alive. Now come."

"Yeah, well, I'm not interested in getting out of Durgaland. I've got a real friend back in that village and I'm going to get her. So, thank you for killing the dragon, now if you'll just point me in the right direction, I'll be going."

He sighed again and walked back to me. "I'm not going to argue with you, son, but if all you want to do is throw your life away after I've saved it, I'm not going to help. You can follow me back to my home, or you can just sit and wait here. Those Treoynn will be back eventually and then you can fight them all by yourself. I'm sure it will be as easy as facing this dragon alone."

He turned and trotted off into the forest. I stood watching him a moment, thinking about what he said, and then took off after him. I was definitely going to need allies to get Lilah out of the Treoynn village alive. If she wasn't already dead.

FIVE

It took maybe a quarter of an hour weaving through the forest to reach a small hut built into the side of a hill. Inside, I was surprised to find the hut was actually just a front for a cave that was twice the size of the hut, creating a roomy living space. The troll obviously lived alone since the entire area was one big room with all his limited possessions scattered about.

"I thought Durgahh were very attached to their clans. Why are you living out here alone?" We hadn't spoken during our jog through the forest, and I was surprised to discover he was a hermit troll.

He ignored my question and extended a hand. "I'm Rikk."

I took the proffered hand, "Betty."

He snorted. "Isn't that a woman's name for you skels?"

"It's a long story."

"I've got time."

"I don't. Look, Rick, we need..."

"Rikk."

"That's what I said, Rick."

"It's Rikk, not Rick."

"I can't tell the difference."

He sighed. "Yeah, well you're not Durgahh."

"And you're not a 'skel,' so why don't we stop discussing names and start discussing how we're going to get my friend away from the Treoynn."

"First tell me why a skel is in Durgaland and why the Treoynn want you dead."

I stared at him and scratched at my beard while considering what to tell him. I decided to keep to the basics. "I'm investigating a potions ring that's distributing overly-strong potions in Ilanerra. I found out the potion ring uses the Treoynn symbol and brought a troll guide to find the clan."

Rick laughed, "Well, congratulations, you found 'em. The Treoynn clan has been making potions for almost as long as I've been alive, which is quite some time, mind you." He shook his finger in my face. "Used to help make the potions for 'em, too; mostly things to grow plants better." He chuckled again, probably remembering the way he trapped and killed the dragon. "'Course, that isn't all they make. But now that you found 'em, so what? They don't distribute the stuff, just make it."

"You mean..."

"I'm afraid your little expedition was for nothing. You found the potion makers, but even if you somehow managed to wipe out the whole clan, the corp across the sea that sells the stuff won't even notice. They've got a dozen clans making potions for 'em, and one less isn't going to matter. And your guide is probably dead." He paused, "Well, maybe since he's Durgahh and you just hired him, they'll just kick him out."

"Her," I corrected.

"You brought a *woman* to guide you?"

"Yeah, what of it? She's a friend and a tech, just like you."

"How much of a friend?"

"None of your business."

"Touchy one, aren't you. You still want to get your lady-friend away from the Treoynn if she's there and alive?"

"Yes. Are you going to help me?"

"I just might. What's in it for me?"

I gazed around the hut/cave. "It looks like you need everything, so what do you want the most."

Rick stared at me for a moment, "A way out of here."

"To where?"

"Anywhere, over in one of your skel cities,

wherever you're from. Look, you got time?"

"Right now I've got all the time you have."

"Ha! So you do. Listen, I told you I used to make potions for the Treoynn?"

I nodded.

"Good." He rubbed his hands together and started pacing. "It was a good job. Like I said, I'm just a nature trollmen. I cast spells to make things grow or to kill plants, like weeds. I told myself the potions were for good and ignored the mean stuff—potions to make people spit fire, or poison them, or make their... 'muscles' bigger. I'm a Durgahh and this was my clan. I kept my head down and did my job and told myself it was just for skels anyway."

He paused for a moment and sat down, putting his hands on his knees and staring at the floor. "Then my daughter expressed, and she had thought powers. I knew what that would mean. They'd use her to make mind-reading potions, mind-control potions, the works. I couldn't just ignore it any more. I decided to run away from the tribe, from Durgaland itself, if I had to."

I can be kind of dumb some—well, a lot of times—but I'm not stupid. I suddenly knew who I was talking to, but I kept my mouth shut and trained my eyes to display no changed awareness

"I told my daughter," he continued, "some story

about being forced to torture people with her powers because I didn't want her questioning why all of a sudden doing the same job I had been doing for years was such a bad thing. We snuck out of the village and headed for my wife's clan, but they wouldn't keep us, so we headed toward a seaport."

Rick sucked in a deep breath to steel himself for what came next. "We got caught by a dragon out in the woods. I distracted it, figuring I would die while my wife and daughter lived. But that's when I discovered that a dragon's mouth is real sensitive to spells. I let it chase me through the woods for a while, knocking down trees to keep it off me. Then I pulled a wand and started throwing spells at it just to try and confuse it a bit. I hit it with a fireball right in the mouth and it screamed and took off running.

"I sat for a bit to let the trembling stop, then took off back toward where I'd left my family, but I couldn't find the right spot. So I headed for Banjall to see if I could meet them there." He sucked air again, and his voice shook a bit as he continued. "I got there just in time to see a bunch of Treoynn dragging my wife's body off the docks. I hid, too broken up to even try to fight 'em. Asked around and found out my little girl had jumped in the ocean and drowned. I spent a few days waiting to see if her body washed up or if maybe she had just hid under the pier and I might find her, but I finally gave her up just as I had to give up my wife."

He stared at me with red-rimmed eyes. "I lost my wife and daughter that day and I decided to come back here and do whatever I could to my old tribe." He paused again and slowly shook his head. "I annoy them. Break up their hunting parties, dissolve pieces of the village wall, steal some of their supplies. But I'm tired and the revenge business is no way to live your life. I'm too old to keep up this nonsense. I'll help you find your lady-friend and then you can take me with you when you go home."

I let the silence stretch out for a while so he could compose himself. He drooped in his seat, a man defeated by life, but who wouldn't quite give up on living. I could tell where Lilah got her determination. Once he seemed calm enough, I asked, "Is your daughter's name, Lilah?"

He started. "Yes, yes it was. How did you know..."

"She's my 'lady-friend.'"

I wasn't quite prepared for the explosion. His charge knocked me back off my stool, but I never hit the ground because he had grabbed me and slammed me against a rock wall.

"My daughter's alive and you brought her back here!" He screamed at me. "What were you thinking, you stupid skel..."

"Shut up!" I yelled at him while grabbing his wrists. A bit of a twist and he was forced to let go and he collapsed.

Falling to his knees and bowing his head to the dirt floor, he sobbed, "She's alive. She's alive." Over and over he repeated himself as he rocked his body. I walked back over to my stool and sat and waited while he collected himself.

He finally stopped rocking and crying and sat cross-legged on the floor and looked up at me. "Tell me. Tell me everything."

I gave him the whole story, from meeting Lilah at her hold to hearing the story of their flight from her perspective to our journey here. He rummaged around for food during the story and I finished as we were eating. Several times during my tale he had grinned broadly at descriptions of his daughter's exploits. By the time I wrapped up, he was all business.

"Well, we know one thing," he said.

"What's that?"

"She's still in the village and still alive. They would never let such a valuable trollmen leave, but they will force her to make their potions."

"Can we get her out?"

He gave me an evil grin, "Son, I've been stealing from the Treoynn for twenty years. She's as good as free." Then his face got serious, "And once we get her out, you and me are gonna have a little chat about my girl."

SIX

"What's the pig for?" I pointed to the large sow we had captured, drugged, and dragged through the woods to our position outside the Treoynn village.

"Remember that dragon you fought?" Rick asked.

"I'll never forget, probably for the rest of my life."

Rick chuckled. "Well, the Treoynn captured a wild pig and staked it out. Dragons have really good hearing and there's always at least a few wandering around the edges of the forest, looking for easy food. One heard the pig squealing and came to get a free meal and the Treoynn brought you there as dessert.

"We're going to do the same thing to them. Once we get Lilahh out, we'll stake the pig out here in the trees and Lilahh can wake it up. Once it starts squealing, a dragon will come investigate and find the village full of Durgahh running around."

"Why will they be running around out here?"

"Because on the way out, I'll dissolve most of one

side of their village wall." Rick's grin was positively maniacal.

"Wait, I don't want to kill them."

"Nobody's going to die, or, very few. Durgahh have been fighting dragons for generations. They'll drive it off or kill it and rebuild. What they won't do is chase us. They'll need every Durgahh on hand to take care of the dragon and fix the village."

"You seem a little blasé about dragons. I thought they were giant killing machines."

"Where did you get that idea?"

"Your daughter, for one."

"Hmmm. Well, I guess my daughter left this country while still young enough to see dragons as terrible monsters. Then she lived among you skels for many years and who knows what kind of stories you people tell. Dragons are animals, that's all, and the Durgahh in this village will drive it off or kill it easy enough."

I sighed, "All right, all right. We'll do it your way."

"Of course we will. Now sit back and relax. We won't go in until several hours after dark."

The two of us dozed a bit through the evening. During the day, Rick had exhausted me with questions about Lilah, but he seemed content now to just sit in peace. Once the sun had been down for a long while, we crept up to the village wall. Rick laid a hand on one of the palisade poles and a chunk of it turned into sawdust. I was standing over him and caught the log as it toppled outward, then Rick dissolved it the rest of the way through and I staggered back a little as the full weight fell on me. The bottom of the log thudded on the ground, earning me a reproving stare from Rick.

The two of us hefted the log and carried it away a short distance, then repeated the exercise with an adjacent log. There was now an opening in the village wall large enough for us to squeeze through. Rick had picked a spot behind the chief's house, and we crept up to the back wall. My job was to find the place where Lilah and I had our rooms. I tried to visualize the interior and led the way toward a pair of windows on the far end of the building.

The windows were shuttered and a bit of jiggling showed they were latched on the inside. Rick ran a finger along the seam between the shutters, dissolving the wood, until he found the catch. Then he dissolved the wood around the catch, and the shutters swung open. He gently pushed the shutters farther apart, and tried to open the window. It was unlocked.

We slid the window up and Rick stuck his head inside. After a moment, he withdrew and whispered, "I can't see or hear anything. Let's go inside."

Rick pulled himself through the window, then stuck his face back outside. "There's a couch right here. Soft landing." He moved away and I hoisted myself through with a bit of grunting and jingling of my armor.

"Shhhh," Rick warned, unnecessarily. We prowled around until I recognized it as Lilah's room; but, it was empty.

"Where would they have taken her?" I asked.

"I don't have a clue," Rick replied. "I've only ever invaded their storerooms, never their houses."

"Do they have a jail?"

"Not really. Durgahh waiting for a tribunal are kept under guard in their own houses."

"So where should we look next?"

Rick was silent for a few moments, then said, "Let's try upstairs. They may have locked her in an upper-floor room to keep her from crawling out the window." He crept over to the door, cracked it open a bit and knelt, listening. "I don't hear anything out in the hall. Let's go."

We moved slowly down the hallway toward the main hall and the staircases leading to the upper floors. "Which way first?" I asked.

"Let's go to the third floor first," Rick whispered back. "The higher, the more secure."

We tiptoed up to the third floor and peered down the halls on both sides of the home. Neither showed any guards, so we went down one flight and didn't see any guards along either of those halls. I followed Rick as he retreated into a corner away from the stairs and the hallways.

He leaned in to whisper in my ear, "I don't want to just go randomly opening doors. Sooner or later we'll wake somebody up and then we'll have the whole village on top of us."

I sat silent for a moment, then had an idea. "Lilah's a telepath. Maybe if I took my hood off and started thinking about her, she'll pick up on it and let us know where she is."

"Will that work while she's asleep?" Rick sounded doubtful.

"I don't know," I said, "but it's worth a shot." I reached up to pull off my hood, and that's when the alarms began to sound. High-pitched wailing echoed throughout the house and I was sure it was being heard all over the village.

"Upstairs! Now!" Rick grabbed my arm and took off for the stairway to the third floor.

We ran quickly as I heard movement in the rooms around us and doors banging open. We reached the third floor without anyone seeing us and Rick flew through the first door we saw. A troll was sitting on the edge of a bed, rubbing his eyes as we ran in, but my fist meeting his face sent him back to sleep.

Rick ran to the window and threw it open and the

shutters outside. "To the roof," he said, as he hauled himself out the window and reached up to grab the edge of the roof above him. I had a harder time squirming out the window and couldn't leverage myself up over the roof edge until Rick grabbed me and heaved upward. As I scrambled up onto the tiles of the roof, I heard noises below.

Both of us lay still as trolls shouted at each other and I could hear them moving around just below us. Soon, banging doors and running feet announced they were heading down and outside.

"They think we jumped down to the ground," Rick said through gritted teeth. "Quick. We have to get into the rafters."

He crawled up near the apex of the roof and began dissolving the clay tiles underneath him. Slipping down as he went, he had soon fashioned a hole through the tiles and the planks of wood under them so we could both crawl into the tight space between the sloped roof and the ceilings of the rooms below.

"We'll have to lay here for a while," Rick said. "A guard probably found the hole we put in the village wall. Hopefully, they'll think we ran out the same hole and will search the forest."

"How long until they give up?"

"Oh, a day or so."

"What? That's crazy, we can't just lay here for a

day."

Rick snorted. "Of course we can't. We'll crawl out in an hour or so, once they've had time to disperse into the woods. Then it's just a matter of dodging their patrols until we get back to my place."

"What about Lilah?"

"I haven't forgotten her!" Rick's voice was tense and angry. "But we can't do anything with the whole village riled up. We'll have to come up with a different plan."

"Well, if we're just going to be lying here in the rafters, maybe I can try to contact her. She would have to be awake by now."

"Ha! That's the truth. Go ahead, son."

I removed my mail coif and tried to 'cast' out my thought, thinking Lilah's name over and over. I sat still for a good quarter of an hour, but got no mental reply. Rick lay quietly the whole time, but grunted when I sighed and pulled the gold-laced hood back over my head.

"Nothing, eh?"

I shook my head, "Not a tingle."

"How does that work, anyway?" Rick asked, pointing at my hood.

"It's gold-threaded, blocks anyone from reading my thoughts."

"Gold blocks spells?"

"Yeah. I guess Durgah mostly use dragon hide?"

"Yep. Crazy stuff you skels come up with. Are you sure my daughter can hear you with that hood off?"

"I'm not sure. I just know she's able to sense me from pretty far away most of the time."

"Well, let's focus on getting out of here and then we'll try to hunt her down another way."

We lay quietly for quite a while longer, then Rick pulled himself back out on to the roof and lay there for a few moments before signaling me to come up. He slowly slid down the roof to near the window we had escaped from, bent over the edge, and swore softly. He crawled back up to me and said, "They closed the shutters. We can't get back in that way."

"We can't jump either. So what now?

"Back into the rafters. We'll have to go through the ceiling."

We pulled ourselves back into our crawlspace and Rick went to work on the ceiling so we could drop into the room below. We crept out into the hall and headed for the staircases around the main hall. Looking down, we saw trolls stationed at the doors leading outside.

"We're not going out that way," Rick said.

"We'll go down one floor and drop from a window." I headed for the top of the stairs and Rick followed.

We sidled along the bannister of the staircase, hoping the guards would not look up. Once on the second floor, we headed down the hall and selected a room midway that led to the back of the building. Listening at the door, we heard nothing and crept in and opened the window and shutters.

The ground was some four lengths below, but letting ourselves down while gripping the windowsill would allow a drop of less than two lengths. I went out first, climbing through the window backwards and slowly letting myself down until I was left dangling by my fingers, which weren't going to hold out long. I dropped the rest of the way and fell backward as I hit. The shock jarred me but didn't hurt.

Rick came out next. He was a good half-length shorter than I and would have a longer distance to fall. But he didn't just drop. Using his innate talent, he punched his feet and hands through the wooden wall of the house and climbed down.

I sighed. "I should have let you come down first."

"You were having so much fun jumping, I didn't want to interrupt."

"You're funny. Let's get out of here."

"Use your wand and slice a hole through the palisade."

"Can't *you* do it?"

"Your wand will be faster. Just stop arguing and do what I say."

I shrugged, pulled out my nature wand and sliced

through the bases of several logs. They collapsed outward with a loud crash and voices cried out from the forest.

Rick was already running toward the trees. "You might want to switch to something more violent!" He shouted over his shoulder as he ran.

I sheathed the nature wand, took out my fire wand, and ran after Rick. Some trolls came pelting out of the trees to our left and I flung a fireball in their general direction. They scattered and most hit the dirt. We got into the trees ahead of them, and Rick paused long enough to turn and direct his attention to two trees. They toppled over and Rick came flying past me. I followed him deeper into the woods, the shouts of trolls echoing around us.

As we ran, I fired random blasts in different directions. I hoped the explosions would distract the trolls and cover the sounds of our escape. We continued running, leaping over fallen logs. I hoped Rick knew where he was going, because I certainly didn't. As we veered around another tree, my feet tangled up in the underbrush and I went rolling. Rick turned and pulled me up, but we saw flashes of movement in the trees off to our left.

I fired into the trees and got answering blasts of fire and ice back. Most missed, but one hit me square in the chest and the impact knocked me off my feet again, even as the spell fizzled on the gold threads in my mail. Rick had ducked behind a fallen log and was focusing on the trees near the Treoynn, trying to grow them fast enough to form a wall. I scuttled over the log as spells hit around me and began taking my time and firing back, trying to actually hit one of the trolls. At least one shot landed directly, based on the screams.

A fireball blew up right in my face, singeing my beard and forcing both of us to burrow down below the log.

"What now?" I asked through clenched teeth.

Rick didn't answer. He just looked at me and shook his head.

"They're going to get behind us," I said. I rolled over and peered into the woods. We had been at this long enough the dark of night had begun to fade into the mist of dawn. I couldn't see any movement, so I started to crawl through the underbrush. Noise beside me confirmed Rick was following my lead.

There was shouting off to my left, so I fired a random fireball in that direction. The two of us continued crawling, trying to stick to areas that had the largest concentration of brush and small trees. After several moments, I stopped and sat up next to a tree. The forest was growing silent; the only shouts I could hear were coming from a great distance.

"I think we lost them," I said.

"Nonsense," he whispered through his teeth. "Troll hunters know how to stay silent. They're close now." Rick pulled himself up by the tree and placed his hands and forehead against the trunk. The tree began to swell quickly. I scrambled back as the roots began popping out of the ground.

"They're going to see that," I whispered.

Rick ignored me. The tree was becoming massive, and now I noticed it was beginning to warp. Rick's hands were shaping it, growing it around us. I hurried to get in close to Rick, pressing up against him as he effectively wrapped us in a wooden cocoon. As the wood of the bole began to close around us, I heard renewed shouts close by. The trolls had seen us and I heard running footsteps pounding outside. One troll actually tried to stick his wand through the remaining space, but I pushed it up and then his arm became trapped in the tree.

"Stop!" I yelled at Rick.

He paused and I heard the tree creak a bit around me. "What? You're concerned for this Durgahh trying to kill you?" The troll outside was screaming and thrashing around, but he could not pull his arm from the opening in the tree.

"A little. But mostly, leaving him here blocks anyone else from getting to us unless they decide to disarm him first." I chuckled at my own joke.

I felt Rick's eyes rolling at my attempt at humor, but he relaxed and the tree didn't grow any more. We were now tight against one another, back-to-back. I was facing toward the opening slit that gave us air and was partially blocked by a troll, whose arm protruded through the slit. I had taken his wand from him, and now tried to worm it into my bandolier to keep it safe. Movement was very limited.

Then a voice started shouting outside. Rick began shouting back. The exchange went on for a good while. Once the conversation ended, I asked Rick what had been said.

"Threats. Bargains. The usual kind of stuff. We're safe, but we're stuck. They know that and they'll probably just wait us out. But the hunter who is trapped with us complicates matters for them." Rick heaved a huge sigh. "Mostly what they want is for us to return Lilahh, or the 'mind trollmen' as they call her. So, our job was a wash last night. She was already gone, and they think we have her."

"So she got out on her own?!" I said with admiration and relief.

"Apparently. I don't exactly have any details, you know." Rick chuckled. "That's my daughter." And he laughed some more.

A couple of hours dragged by. The hole in the tree began to feel more like a tomb than sanctuary. I was hot, I was tired, and I suddenly realized I desperately needed to relieve myself. I grumbled at Rick, "Can't you at least make this place bigger?"

"If I make it too much larger, the tree will not be able to support its own weight and it will collapse, probably crushing us. We're like rot in the base of the tree, and we can't 'eat' any more of it."

"Well, as much as I liked your idea at first, I'm thinking we're going to have to give up and try to bust our way out. We can't stay here much longer."

Rick let out a huge sigh. "I know. I've already wet my pants once since we closed ourselves in here."

I cackled. I'd like to say I laughed or chuckled, but it was definitely a cackle. "Good thing our sweat disguises the stench. Look, we can't go out, how about going up?"

"What?"

"Let's climb up through the middle of the trunk, at least a couple lengths, and open up a firing slit. Sort of like a homemade, wooden castle. They won't be able to get a good target firing up at an angle, but they'll be wide open to me. Once I chase them off, we can blow our way out of here and make for your home."

"We might bring the tree down."

"Yeah, but we're going to die if we stay in here, and we'll die if we just try to fight our way out. We've got to take the chance."

"Alright. Rotate with me so I'm closer to the opening."

We sidled around, still back-to-back, so Rick was facing the slit he had left in the tree. I heard him laugh and then the troll still stuck started yelling.

"What did you do?"

"I tickled him." And then I felt dust falling on my head. I began to sneeze as the sawdust clogged up my nostrils. I tried to breathe through my mouth, but that was ten times worse, especially since I was already parched. I began to choke.

"Work up some saliva and spit it out!" Rick admonished. His voice was already above me.

I tried. My throat was dry and I felt like I had no moisture left in my body, but I began swirling my tongue around my teeth, and worked up enough spit to rinse my mouth out. Rick's body was no longer behind me, and with the extra room, I pulled my arm up and began to breathe through my sleeve.

Finally, Rick dropped back down, squeezing against me once more. "Turn around. I'll boost you up. There are hand and footholds up about two lengths and then an opening in the trunk. You'll need your wand out now and keep it above you, if you want to be able to point it out the hole."

I twisted around and pulled my knee up. Rick got under me and I took my fire wand in one hand and reached up with the other and found a "rung" that Rick had carved out of the inside of the tree. I could see sunlight pouring in through a fairly broad hole quite a way above me. I pulled myself up by my hands until my feet could find purchase and then climbed the rest of the way to my firing slit.

The space wasn't ideal. I had to hold my wand hand almost right in front of my face in order to both see and fire through the slit. But I could do it and what I saw filled me with joy. It was going to be even easier than I thought.

A group of six trolls was simply sitting a few lengths away from the tree. They appeared to be bored and at least a couple were dozing. I aimed right in the middle of the group and hit them with a fireball. I kept shooting as they screamed and scattered. At least two were down—unconscious or dead, I couldn't tell—from my first salvo. The other four were running as fast as they could in all directions.

"Let's go!" I shouted downward. I let myself down rapidly as Rick broadened the opening. The trapped hunter didn't bother to stay and fight, but ran after his brothers as soon as he could pull his arm free. Rick and I squeezed out of the tree trunk and ran. Behind, I could hear an ominous creaking sound.

"It's going to come down!" Rick shouted, and increased his pace.

With a giant, cracking boom, the tree keeled over. I glanced over my shoulder to see the tree tear itself apart at the place where we had sheltered and it toppled into the forest, mercifully away from us. It took down a lot of other trees, leaving a swath of destruction on the forest floor. I could feel tremors in my feet as it hit the ground.

SEVEN

We reached Rick's hut without further incident. Neither of us spoke; we just collapsed on the floor. Eventually, Rick found some water and food and we ate in silence. After we ate, we cleaned ourselves up, rolled up in blankets, and went to sleep. We hadn't said a word since running away from our tree cocoon.

We slept most of the day and it was dark outside when I awoke. Rick was already stirring, preparing something to eat. We sat cross-legged on the floor around a low table, eating and talking.

"Lilah's already escaped from the Treoynn. Knowing her, she's probably headed straight back to the Burkahh."

Rick nodded around a mouthful of food. "I'd say that's a good assumption. We aren't going to be able to get within shouting distance of the Treoynn demesne for a month. They're too riled up."

"I wish we had done something about their potion-making operation. I feel like this entire trip has been one huge disaster."

"Eh, we put a dent in production. It will be all-hands to repair the village over the next several days, and nightly patrols will leave everyone too tired to work a lot for another month. Still, like I told you before, these potions are being made for a skel corporation; and, they've got other tribes doing the same thing. They'll hardly notice the absence."

"Why are the trolls—I mean Durgahh—doing this? What interest do they have in helping humans?"

Rick rubbed his jaw. "You may as well say 'troll,' skel." He let out a bitter chuckle. "The Durgahh are selling themselves out, and I'm not sure we're worthy of the name any more. Life is harsh in Durgaland. It's cold and dark most of the year, and the dragons keep us from clearing out more land for growing food and raising animals. But we thought we were doing fine, until we started to get a taste of all the trollmen goods you skels are producing."

"Tech. We call it 'tech,'" I interrupted.

"Whatever. Wands, floaters, lamps, cooking pots...You know what stew tastes like simmered over an open flame?"

I shook my head.

"It tastes like ash. When the corps started trading with us, we couldn't get your 'tech' fast enough. But all we had to trade was lumber, and we weren't going to start chopping down trees for you skels because that leaves us open to the dragons."

Rick paused, gathering his thoughts. "Durgahh trollmen have been making potions for centuries. I guess that's one spell you skels hadn't figured out yet. So we traded potions for tech, and the corps liked it. Liked it enough to demand more, and whole tribes turned to potions as a way of life." Rick shook himself. "Yeah, life was harsh, but it was good. I don't think life is even good here anymore."

"How long have the tribes been making potions for the corporations?"

"Not as long as I've been alive, though I've been alive for quite a while." Rick shook his finger in my face to emphasize his last point. "I can still remember what it was like before we sold our souls to the devil."

I stood up. "Well, I think it's time we went back to Ilanerra and had a chat with the devil. Maybe if we shut down the distribution, the Durgahh can get their souls back."

Rick shook his head, "I wouldn't count on it, son. People who've sold their soul to the devil tend to stay bought."

"You're a pessimist, which is, strangely, quite reassuring. Let's pack everything up and make for the Burkahh demesne. Hopefully, we'll find Lilah, reintroduce you two, and then get a ship back to Fisk."

"It won't be that easy."

"After being stuck in that tree, everything else will be easy."

We decided sleeping the day away was a good thing, as Treoynn were less likely to be patrolling the woods at night. Rick had almost nothing, so we packed mostly food and left the hut open, "For another Durgahh to use," as Rick put it.

When we reached the Burkahh demesne, Rick persuaded the gate guard to guide us to Lilah's grandmother's house. The poor woman recognized her thought-to-be-dead son-in-law and promptly fainted, which didn't endear us to the rest of the family. But, once she was revived, she and Rick cried together for a while, and the rest of the family was ordered to make us comfortable and provide us—especially Rick—with clean clothes.

According to Rick's mother-in-law, Lilah had come through only two days before we arrived, telling how I, her skel 'bodyguard,' had been killed and she left immediately to return to Banjall, and hire a boat back to Ilanerra. We wanted to leave immediately, but grandma wasn't having it. She fussed over Rick and pestered him with questions, all while we were chafing to catch up to Lilah.

We stayed overnight with grandmother, but were

adamant we had to leave as soon as possible to catch up with Lilah. Finally, after another hour of arguing with us, she let us leave for Banjall. We pushed through the two-day journey in only a little more than a day. As we approached the port, I pulled Rick off the road.

"What...?"

"Be quiet," I shushed him. "First, we've got a problem. I spotted a Treoynn standing at the gate. I hope he didn't notice us, but I want to wait here and be sure."

"How could you see his badge from out here?"

"I didn't see his badge, I saw his face. He's the one who handed me a spear when we went dragon hunting."

"Oh."

"Second, we've got a bigger problem. I don't have any money."

"What?"

"When I went out to fight the dragon, I wore my armor and carried my wands. I left all my other possessions in my room in the chief's house. We've got no money to stay at an inn and no money to hire a ship back to Fisk."

Rick worked his jaw a bit while rubbing his palms with his fingers. "OK, let's go take care of the Treoynn you saw and get his vest and badge. Then I'll take care of the ship. If we're fast enough about it, we won't have to stay in Banjall at all, so no need for an inn."

"But what about searching for Lilah?"

"We know she came here looking for a ship home. We'll just have to assume she got there. If Treoynn are keeping an eye on the harbor, we can't spend any time snooping around. We've got to get away from here."

I sighed, but I knew he was right. "All right, let's wait out here until that Treoynn heads away from the gate, and then we'll track him until we get a chance to ambush him."

Rick sat on the ground, while I leaned against the trunk of a tree and watched the troll at the gate. After an hour or so, he left and headed into the city. We moved fast, coming out of the trees at a trot and heading for the gate. As a port city, Banjall's gates were unguarded and wide open and we passed into the town unchallenged. The troll we were after was a few blocks ahead of us, and striding quickly.

I picked up the pace to close some distance and Rick had to trot to keep up. The troll hung a right and I hurried to make it around the corner, forgetting to look around the corner first. I had definitely been out of the city for too long. The troll was standing in front of me as I came around the corner, a wand pointed directly at me and two friends with him. I halted and put my hands up. The troll growled something at me, and I shook my head looking back at Rick for a translation.

Rick wasn't there. I started and the troll said something to me again. I tried to shrug while keeping my hands in the air. One of the other trolls, with a heavy accent, said, "Where is Durgahh? One lives in forest."

"Your guess is as good as mine," I replied. Seeing the somewhat blank stare, I simplified, "I do not know."

The trolls muttered among themselves, and then a large chunk of wood fell from the sky and brained the troll with the wand. The other two shouted and jumped, and I jumped as well, right at one of the two, delivering a flying kick to his groin. He doubled over and I slammed my knee into his face. He dropped, and I turned to the other troll, but he was already running away.

I looked up and saw a large chunk missing from the roof of the building next to me, and Rick peering over the edge. "Good shot," I shouted up at him.

"Keep it down," he said, "and grab that vest."

Trolls around me were stopped and staring, and a few began shouting as I rolled over my erstwhile spear-sharing friend and stripped him of his tribal vest. I tucked my prize under my arm and hurried into an alley between two buildings and Rick slipped down from the roof above me.

"Let me have that," he ordered as he reached for the vest. He pulled it on and trotted down the alley. He kept to alleyways, turning randomly, occasionally cutting through gardens, always changing course until we were well away from the scene of the fight. Then he moved out onto a main street and looked around to get his bearings.

"It's been twenty years since I was here," he said. "Where are the ships docked?"

I looked around. "I can't tell. I've only been through here once myself and this doesn't look familiar. Just ask somebody."

Rick shrugged and accosted a couple of pedestrians until he got one who pointed us toward the docks. We made good time, and strode along the piers until we reached the area that had large warehouses built up against the water. Rick pulled on his vest to straighten it, stood a little taller, and then strode confidently along the dock. We passed a couple of ships where trolls were loading or unloading cargo, and then we saw some loading crates with the Treoynn symbol on them.

Rick marched up to the laborers and barked some questions. One of them called out to someone on board the ship and a human walked out on deck. "What is it?" She demanded.

Rick looked up at her and announced, "I'm a messenger from the Treoynn. My porter and I need to travel with this shipment."

The captain stared at Rick for a moment, then threw up her hands. "Yeah, OK. Come on."

As we boarded, I whispered to Rick, "Just like that?"

"Yes. These captains are paid well by the corps to carry shipments for the tribes, and the tribes use them to send Durgahh back-and-forth to the skel lands as well. I never got to go over the Straights, but I knew many who had. The captain will feed us, but otherwise we just stay out of her way."

"The captain will feed you," I sighed, remembering that my nausea bands were back in my pack in the Treoynn village. "I'll be out of everyone's way being sick."

EIGHT

The passage over the Durgahh Straights was uneventful, except I couldn't keep food down and had trouble even keeping myself hydrated. Fortunately, the trip was only a couple of days and the boat was going to Fisk. I thought we were lucky to get a boat going where we needed to be, but Rick told me almost every ship from Banjall went to the closest "skel" port, which happened to be Fisk. From there it was cheaper for the corps to ship potions overland.

After disembarking, I started looking around for a bank. We had come into a port used for cargo, not passengers, and I wasn't familiar with the area. Rick followed me silently, gawking at the sight of a big city for the first time in his life. We walked between warehouses, dodging freight floaters until coming out on a main thoroughfare. I recognized the street, and could tell, by looking toward the skyscrapers in the high-rent district, about where we were in Fisk.

I led Rick across the street and headed in the general direction of downtown until we found a market. Looking around, I spied a bank. The changers gave me funny looks as I walked in with a troll trailing behind me, and looking as though I hadn't washed or cleaned my clothes in days, which was true.

I stood in line until a changer was free. "I need to access my account," I said.

"Certainly, sir." The changer slid a pad toward me and I placed my hand on the smooth metal plate. I felt the tingle as my thoughts were probed and my identity confirmed.

"What can I get for you, Mr. Sterling?"

"I need an exchequer card, please."

"Just a moment, sir." The changer went into a back room and returned a moment later with a small metal disk imprinted with the bank's logo. He gripped the disk in one hand while touching the other to the ID plate. Once he had melded my account information into the disk, he handed it to me. I thanked him and we walked out.

"What was that all about?" queried Rick.

"That was a bank. The corps run them so people have easy access to their money whenever they need it. The changers are all telepathic melders who can imprint your personal account info along with the bank's authorization, and then you use the disk to pay for things. As long as you have money in your account, of course."

"How does the disk know when you run out of money?"

"It doesn't. It just has my account info. When I use it, the person I'm paying uses a tell hooked to the bank, the tell reads my account info, checks the money in my account, and then lets the seller know whether I have enough money or not."

"That's how you skels do money?" Rick shook his head. "So a corp holds all your money, and knows everything you spend it on. And you think this is a good idea?"

I shrugged. "It works. Come on, we'll get a floater to my apartment. I need some food. And a bath. And clean clothes. Wouldn't hurt you either."

Crossing town to my apartment in the tanning district took only a half hour. Before heading up to my apartment, I went down a block to a restaurant and ordered takeout.

Rick didn't ask any more questions until we were in my flat, but then the spout opened.

While we ate, we discussed banks, restaurants, running water, and the smell from the tanneries near my apartment. After dinner I showed him how to work the shower and found some clothes for him to wear. They would be too big, but would do until we could get the clothes from the Burkahh cleaned.

"Where do we go from here?" Rick asked as I exited the shower. I stepped behind a screen to get dressed while I answered. "In the morning we'll go to the place Lilah was staying in The Caverns—the part of town where the trolls live."

"Why don't you just call her? She can hear you now, right?"

I sighed. "My apartment is shielded. And I don't want to step outside unshielded because of 'paths everywhere trying to spy on people. I know in Durgaland there aren't a lot of techs, and so you haven't built up quite the defenses we have. Around here, people protect themselves at all times. We'll find Lilah the old-fashioned way. If she made it back to Fisk, she'll probably go straight back to her cousin. If she's not there and her cousin hasn't heard from her, then we'll start asking questions around the docks. We might go see Cristof as well."

"Who is Cristof?"

"My employer. Lilah knows him as well; he helped her with loans while she was struggling with a problem in her hold. He seems to have his eye on a lot of things at once. Maybe he's heard from her or knows where she's at. Once we've found Lilah, we'll hook up with Jewels and Sam and track down the corp that's paying for the potions."

"Jewels and Sam?"

I smiled. "Friends of mine. Jewels is an elf and Sam is an ogre. I have a feeling we'll need their help to track down the potion ring. But, that's enough for one night. Let's get some sleep."

"All right, but once we find Lilahh, I'm going to teach you how to pronounce both our names correctly."

The next morning, we headed for The Caverns, and I realized I had no idea how to find my way back to Lilah's cousin's house. I found my way to the alchemist where I first bumped into Lilah, but then I couldn't remember where to go. I had been so intent on following her, I hadn't paid any attention to which streets she took home.

Rick was staring around at the dank alleyways and filthy trolls trudging through them and his lips curled up in disgust. "How do they live this way? Don't they have any pride?"

"I don't think pride has anything to do with it," I said. "I think they do this to be left alone. Hardly anyone other than trolls come in here; hardly anyone *wants* to come in here."

"I can't believe I've spent the past twenty years wishing I were here. I'd take my hut any day."

"Their houses look much nicer on the inside. This really is a façade to keep non-trolls away." I growled in frustration. "And right now, it's keeping me from finding my way around." I turned slowly in circles, trying to get my bearings. "Now if I could just spot something familiar..."

"You're lost?" he interrupted.

"Yeah. I was following your daughter and not paying attention to where we were going."

"You said Lilahh was living with a cousin. Do you remember the cousin's name?"

I wracked my brain. "Ummm...Alan. Yeah, I think that's it."

"Did you mean Alinn?"

"Probably, yeah. Let's not go through that again."

Rick huffed and accosted a troll walking past. They spoke briefly, and Rick headed off down the street. He kept stopping random passerby and asking them questions and running off down side streets until I was thoroughly lost again. Eventually we ended up in front of a door that could have been Alinn's, but I wasn't sure and said as much.

"Well, this is where my informants told me he lives. So, in we go," Rick opened the door and pushed me through. The room certainly looked like the foyer of Alinn's place, but probably every troll house had the same kind of entrance. I reached up and pulled on the lamp, but nothing happened. Rick looked at me.

"A trapdoor is supposed to open from the ceiling. I

can see the outline of it, but it's not opening."

"Perhaps they locked it."

"Maybe, but they hadn't locked it the last time...oh, I was so close behind Lilah, they didn't have time to seal it."

"So, how do we knock?"

"I don't know..."

As I spoke, a voice called out from above us, "Who's there?"

"It's Betty. Betty Sterling. You know, Lilah's friend."

There was silence for a moment, then the trapdoor banged down and Lilah's face appeared. "Betty!" She squealed. I'd like to say it differently, but it was a squeal. "You're alive!"

I started climbing the ladder, "Yeah, it takes more than dragons to shut me..." I had reached the top and she dragged me off the ladder and hugged me fiercely while sobbing into my chest.

"I was sure you were dead. I had no choice but to run home. And now you've come back to me."

I could feel myself blushing. "Yes, I'm alive and I'm here. And I have someone else with me." I gently disengaged her arms and turned her toward Rick, who had climbed up behind me and was staring at her in stunned silence. I never thought I could actually see a male troll go pale under his fur and beard, but Rick was pale.

Lilah turned, still sniffling, "Who is thi…"

There was a long, long pause.

"Daddy?" It was a breath, almost too faint to hear, as though a 12-year old girl was whispering from across two decades. Rick just nodded, tears streaming down his face.

"Daddy!" This time it was a primal scream, wrenched from Lilah's soul. She threw herself on Rick, weeping loudly and Rick wrapped himself around her and said, "My little girl," over and over.

I decided to make myself comfortable on the divan while they got themselves under control. Alinn had decided to vacate the room altogether. The reunion lasted quite a while, until Lilah finally managed to push herself away.

"Why didn't you come find me?" Lilah's voice was still full of tears, but also sounded a bit angry.

"I tried," Rick sobbed. "The people in town told me you were dead, that you had drowned." He took a deep breath. "I saw your mother's body, and I couldn't take any more, so I ran away. I'm so sorry, Lilahh."

She reached out to stroke his cheek, her voice softer, but still sad. "It's OK, Daddy. It's OK." She turned to look at me. "How did you find him?"

"Well," I said, "it's more like he found me. He's the one who kept me from being a dragon's dinner. What's more to the point, is how did you get away?"

"Those idiot trolls," I started at her use of the derogative name for her people, "they didn't have enough sense to wear protective headgear, so I read their thoughts as they returned. I let them console me over your death, and then snuck out as soon as it was dark. Their guards were easily distracted, and I just ran back home. Oh, wait here."

Lilah ran off down the hall, and returned a moment later with my pack. "I brought all your things with me; I was going to give them to Joshua."

"Thank you. Thank you very much. What are you grinning at?" I asked Rick, who was standing with a big smile on his face.

"Nothing," he replied. "I'm just happy to have my Lilahh again."

We spent the morning catching up on more recent events. After lunch, I excused myself and left father and daughter to reconnect. It was time to get back to work.

NINE

I pushed open the door of room 316 and walked into the crowded waiting room. Every time I came to Cristof's office, it was always crowded and always different people. There were humans, trolls, ogres, elves, and several types of people—or creatures—I couldn't name. Cristof's office was always crowded, and, yet, I had never had to wait.

Today was no exception. I hadn't been in the room long enough to find a seat when an elf strode up to me and said my name. I looked down at his head near my kneecap and admitted I was Betty Sterling.

"Mr. Cristof will see you now," he said, striding off toward the door to Cristof's office.

"Hey! Wait! I haven't even announced myself yet!"

The elf turned at the door. "Mr. Cristof knows you're here. Please come along."

I hurried after him and entered Cristof's office. It was just as small and barren as ever. Nothing more than Cristof sitting at a table, his trim, brown beard matching perfectly with a ponytail of hair hanging down his back.

He stood and shook my hand as I sat down. "How are you today, Betty?"

"I'm fine. How did you even know I was here? How did you get me in so quickly when I hadn't even asked to see you?"

Cristof chuckled, "I knew you'd be coming 'round today and cleared some space in my schedule."

"But what about all those other people waiting? They look like they've been here a long time, yet you move me right to the front of the line."

"Now, now, Betty. Don't worry your head about them, they'll all be taken care of. Let's get to what brings you here."

I gushed out everything I had learned about the potion ring and the events in Durgaland. Cristof took it all in, his fingers steepled in front of his face, almost completely motionless. When I finished with the events of that morning, he heaved a deep sigh and flattened his hands on the table.

"You've bit off a big mouthful, Betty, if you're going after a corporation."

"You hired me to put a stop to the overpowered potions. That's what I mean to do."

Cristof leaned back in his chair and crossed his

arms. "I admire your zeal, but I want you to understand just what you're up against. Do you?"

"Yeah, the corps run everything in Fisk. They run everything in Ilanerra, almost. They run the banks, run the police, build roads, even hire judges and manage the courts. They employ just about everyone, but their main business is keeping the peace and making sure everyone is taken care of. I'm having trouble wrapping my head around the fact they are also the ones pushing potions on the public."

"But of course they are," Cristof said. "Look, Betty, one of my purposes in hiring you was to set you free of the system. So, it's time you learned exactly what the system is. Come over here."

Cristof stood and went over to a window. Strangely, I had never noticed the window before. A little bemused, I went and stood by the window with him.

"Tell me what you see."

"The city," I shrugged. "Flyers traveling the streets, and people walking on the sidewalks. Shops, businesses, restaurants. All the usual."

"What you're looking at," Cristof began, "is an entity. Not living like you, or me, but it has a type of life. Each person down there is one little part of the greater whole. The corporations are the brains of this entity. The people who control those organizations control every part of the body. All the people you see moving around out there are at the beck and call of one person—their ultimate boss."

Cristof went back to the table and I sat across from him once more. "The boss of each corporation has one goal, and only one...acquiring wealth. They can only do that as long as the individuals in their employ cooperate in producing wealth. Now, if you want someone to do something for you, how would you go about getting them to do so willingly?"

"I'd pay them."

"Yes, but that's just the beginning. After all, I pay you, right?" Cristof grinned at me and I began to feel a little queasy. "If all you do is pay someone, then you only control them for the duration of that one job. But what if you want them to get up every day, day after day, and work for you? Do you think a paycheck alone would keep people doing exactly what you want?"

"Maybe?" I was unsure of where Cristof was going. A paycheck had always seemed enough to me, but seeds of doubt were creeping in.

Cristof continued. "If you want people to give their lives to you, you must make those lives palatable, but only as long as the people continue to serve you. So you provide for their protection and safety. Against who? Against those who step out of line.

"The murderers and thieves, certainly, but also

those who dare to speak out against the corporations. Those who want to act independently, rather than live according to the dictates of the corporation. In all those years of working over people, did you ever stop to wonder what their crimes were?"

I squirmed in my seat. I didn't like being reminded of my past as a corp enforcer. "In that line of work, I didn't ask questions. I assumed most were late on payments."

Cristof sighed. "Yes, some were late on payments, and did they deserve to have you wreck their shop, or break their leg, simply for being late? And some had nothing to do with money. Some of their crimes involved not buying from the 'right' supplier, or refusing to serve a particular customer, or not buying corporation insurance for their business.

"In a living entity like this city, anyone who gets out of line is a cancer, one that must be brought in line or cut out of the body. But..." Cristof paused for a moment. "But, you can't just go around beating people up or throwing them in prison. No, if you did that, people would begin to resent their place in the body and try to break free. So, the corporations also distract them. Sports, psycasts, taverns, even potions. If you keep the people comfortable and entertained, they won't rebel. Rebellions are built on dissatisfaction and want; if people are satisfied and well-fed, they will keep doing exactly what you tell them to do."

My queasiness had settled into a lump in my throat, especially when he talked about why I had been paid to punish people. I didn't want to buy his vision of life. "So, what are you telling me? That the corps pay people well and keep the peace, but maybe do some shady stuff here and there? And that's supposed to be a bad thing?"

Cristof's eyes bored into mine. "I'm saying that paying people well and keeping the peace may be the shadiest 'stuff' of all. It keeps people in line and keeps them from questioning their life. As long as they do their job and keep their mouth shut, the corp will take care of them..."

"And this is a bad deal?"

"The corp will take care of them," Cristof repeated, "until it doesn't anymore. So long as they remain healthy, and compliant, and are useful, they live what they think is the good life. Then they cease being useful, and the corp casts them aside. Or they try to show a little independence and the corp sends you to beat some sense into them. They're chained to the corp."

"I'm not getting this. You're saying the people who can work whatever job they want, take the vacations they want, enjoy the entertainment they want, aren't free?"

Cristof ticked off my objections one by one. "They can't work whatever job they want, only jobs approved by the corporations and taught in the corporate-run schools. They can only vacation to corporate-approved places. They only get the entertainment the corporation gives them. I am not suggesting one should use one's freedom to drink oneself to death. But how is drinking from the corporate well any different?"

"What did you really hire me to do, Mr. Cristof?"

"I want you to break one of the controls the corporations have over the people. The potion rings affect not just the people here in Fisk, but all over Ilanerra, and the Durgahh across the sea. They're becoming greedy and pushing ever more powerful potions on the public. We—you, must stop them."

"This has become a much scarier job."

"Fear is a powerful motivator. What do you fear more, Betty? The corporations, or a life enslaved by them?"

I looked at him for a long time. "I'm going to need money to buy help."

Ten

"Who is it?"

"Betty."

The door opened and I found myself face-to-face with Jewels. She preferred living in a human-sized apartment and was levitating herself up to face me.

"Well, look who the cat let go."

"What's that supposed to mean?"

"I know you've been hanging out with the troll. I've got friends on the docks who told me you two took a trip to troll country. Was it a nice honeymoon?"

"Shut up, Jewels, and let me in. I've got business to discuss."

"What makes you think I'm free?"

"If I have a job, are you going to turn me down?"

"No," Jewels sulked. She floated aside and I strode in and sank into an overstuffed armchair. Jewels perched atop a stool, keeping us at eye level. Unlike most elves, she went out of her way to make human visitors feel comfortable.

"First, Lilah and I are NOT married. We went to Durgaland on business. Second, we need your help to finish the job."

"Give me the picture."

I pulled off my gold-threaded coif and let my mind wander over the events of the past couple of months. I could feel Jewels's mind flitting around the edges of my thoughts as she absorbed the information.

"Wow. OK, that's freaky. Dragons? The cat's father? Corps getting trolls to make potions? Instead of asking what you've been doing, I should ask what you haven't been doing. It would take less time."

I opened my eyes and leaned forward. Jewels was resting her arms on her legs and slowly shaking her head back and forth as she tried to let everything sink in.

"We've got to put a stop to the potion rings in Fisk."

"You don't know what you're asking, Betty. If the corps really are behind this, we're begging to be killed. You don't cross the corps."

"Someone has to, sometime, or they just keep doing whatever they want to people. What if it's one of your friends that gets a juiced potion and blows up?"

"That's not fair, Betty. My friends don't do potions."

"So you think, but do you know? And what does it matter if it's not your friends getting hurt? Do other people not deserve help?"

"It has nothing to do with whether other people need help, it has everything to do with whether I am the one to help them, and I say I'm not."

"Okay," I shrugged. "Let's make this a simple matter of business. You help me, I pay you. Forget about helping others, at least you'll be helping yourself."

"You can't pay me enough to go against the corps."

"How does 500 marks sound?"

Her eyes went wide. "What's the plan? And are we getting Sam in on the deal?"

"I'm meeting him in a couple of hours at The Thundercloud. Wanna' go with?"

"Oh, really?" Jewels sighed. "I hate that place, but, yeah, alright."

I left Jewels and went for something to eat. The last place I wanted to buy food was The Thundercloud, so I made sure I was full before heading uptown to The Market. Fisk has lots of little markets around, and various shops and restaurants are scattered all over town; but, there's only one Market, with a capital 'M.'

The Market takes up several city blocks just north of the Downtown business sector, where all the corps have their headquarters. It's full of pubs, and eateries, and shops—mostly high-end stuff. A little armory nestled in a corner had sold me my gold-threaded mail and hood. I sighed as I realized I was probably going to have to replace them. My adventures in Durgaland had not been kind to my clothing—especially my armor.

The Thundercloud was a bistro that set itself apart not by the food it served, but by a bit of tech that kept the inside under a constant threat of storm. The ceiling seemed to be non-existent, and dark clouds roiled and seethed while lightning flitted among them and thunder was almost constantly rolling.

The worst part was when it actually rained. Each table had an umbrella over it, but that only served to keep your food semi-dry. Water pouring off the umbrella combined with the rain to drench the diners. But, people loved it. Especially kids, who thought eating in the rain was the coolest thing in the world.

I shook my head and glanced over at Sam. He was singing and playing some kind of percussion instrument. It was shaped vaguely like a guitar, but covered with buttons, and his fingers flew over the device, tapping rhythmically and producing a wide variety of sounds. It was really quite lovely. I sat back and enjoyed the show, while fending off a waiter who wanted to take my order.

By the end of Sam's set, Jewels had joined me. She sat on the table, as close to the base of the umbrella as possible, and was busy chewing on something that looked like raw fish mixed with rice. Sam put his instrument inside a case, brought it with him, and slid it under the table to keep it out of any rain.

The Thundercloud could accommodate ogres, but we had a human-sized table, so Sam had to sit cross-legged on the floor and duck his head under the edge of the umbrella. About that moment it began to rain. Sam said not a word about the water sheeting down his back, but Jewels and I instinctively hunched over, and I crowded into the edge of the table to get more of me under cover.

"How ya' doing, Sam?"

"Tolerable. I assume you arranged this meeting because you have another job?"

"Yes, but first, why don't you tell me about your new toy." I toed the instrument case under the table.

Sam's eyes lit up. "It is called a finger-drum; a new piece of tech a group of elves in the Conclave just thought up." He rubbed his hands together. "Each button on the device is linked to a sound box. When I tap a button, the sound box produces a particular sound. Some of the buttons produce typical drum sounds, while others produce bell-like tones at various pitches. It is almost like having a complete band in my hands."

"It sounds wonderful," I offered. Sam beamed at

the compliment.

I continued, "Look, do you mind waiting for a little? Lilah and her father are supposed to be coming."

"Her father?"

"It's a long story."

"Were you planning on talking about something else while we waited?"

I sighed. "No, you're right. Okay, it started a couple of months ago..."

I had just gotten to the fight with the dragon when Lilah and Rick showed up. The rain had stopped by then, but the umbrella was still dripping, so they pulled their chairs in close. Unlike me, no one else seemed to have compunctions about eating food that might get soaked, so while they ordered and got their food, I finished catching Sam up on recent events.

"So, I assume we are going to shut down the potion ring?"

"Yeah. Wait, Lilah, can you make sure we're warded?"

She smiled at me. "I was going to do it as soon as we came in, but Jewels already had one up."

I started guiltily. "Oh. I forgot to ask..."

"It's okay, Betty," Jewels said in an overly sweet voice, "I'm watching out for you. Somebody has to."

"Thank you, Jewels," I said a little acerbically. "Let's get down to details. We're going to have to trace the chain backward. We know where it's going out, and we know where it's coming in, what we don't know is who is connecting the two and controlling the whole operation.

"Rick, I want you to head for the docks. Put on that Treoynn vest we brought with us, and try to find a cargo that's just come in. Insert yourself into the process of moving it off the docks and getting it to the suppliers. Take Jewels with you. She can nudge people's minds so they trust you and warn you if anyone gets suspicious."

"You're making me work with the cat?" Jewels complained.

"I'm paying you to do what I tell you. Suck it up and do your job." Jewels reared back, startled at my tone, but said nothing. "Lilah, start with the alchemy shop near where we first bumped into each other. Act as a buyer and try to get the shopkeeper to order 'something special.' I'll give you enough money to wave in his face to keep him from asking questions. Take Sam with you as a bodyguard. I'm going to shadow you and try to track the shopkeeper back to his runners and then track them until, hopefully, I meet up with Rick and Jewels.

"Once we have the locus where the supply meets distribution, we can work our way up the chain to the person pulling the strings. Any questions?"

"Can't Lilahh and I work together?" Rick asked.

"I get it. You just found each other after twenty years, but this is a Durgahh system of supply and distribution. You two need to be the leads at each end."

Rick nodded.

Sam spoke up. "Would it not be more prudent to have Jewels work with Lilahh while I guard Rikk on the docks?" I noticed the slight emphasis on Rick's name and saw his pleased reaction. Looked like I was the only one who didn't know how to pronounce troll names. "Once Lilahh has baited the shopkeeper, Jewels would be able to assist you in tracking the runners."

"It's a good idea, Sam, but that's putting our only two telepaths on the same team. We need a telepath at the docks, plus Jewels has enough firepower to help Rick if he needs it."

Lilah laid her hand on my arm. "It's a good plan, Betty. When do we start?"

"First thing tomorrow," I said. "Everybody get a good night's sleep...After you dry out, of course."

At my words, it started to rain again.

ELEVEN

Just hanging around outside a shop, especially in The Caverns, would have looked very suspicious. I arranged through Cristof to have work done on the street near the potion shop, and joined the crew pulling up pavers and putting down new ones. Unfortunately, blending in with the work crew meant leaving my armor behind, but I was still warded against telepathy by a neck chain given me by Lilah.

She and Sam had been and gone at least an hour when a troll I hadn't seen before came slouching down the street. I recognized the Treoynn badge on his vest, and watched as he turned into Alkym. I kept mechanically working on the job, waiting for him to come out. Once he did, I gave him a block's lead and then walked away from my work and followed him down the street. The others working paid me no mind; they had been paid well to ignore me.

Tracking someone through a city is a complicated

job, especially if they are alert to the possibility. You can't exactly mirror their movement; people get alarmed quickly when someone else stops and starts at exactly the same time as they. The trick is to vary your pace. I kept steadily moving in the same direction as my target, but slowed and quickened my pace randomly. People watching for a tail tend to look at a spot rather than at the general population; since I was always in a different position in the crowd, he never noticed me specifically.

The troll turned several times, winding his way through The Caverns. The extra turns made it more difficult to keep up with him. He left The Caverns uptown near the business district. Once into the main part of Fisk, the troll made a beeline northeast, passing through the heart of the skyscrapers housing the corporations Cristof said were probably employing him. I expected him to turn aside into one of the office complexes, but he kept going.

We cleared the skyscrapers and the troll approached the Triangle. The Triangle is Fisk's main Tricrosse arena. Hundreds of years ago, our ancestors played a game where two teams attempted to score points by throwing a small ball into nets using only long sticks with baskets on the end. Somewhere along the way, an amateur league with too many teams turned the rectangular field into a triangle and had three teams playing against each other. The change proved so popular, Crosse morphed into Tricrosse and went professional.

Fisk's Triangle was unique among Tricrosse arenas in that it was actually built in the shape of a triangle. Most Tricrosse arenas are circular or oval and only the playing field has three sides. The troll ambled across the empty floater lot and headed down a ramp into a loading area. I had stayed outside the lot since it was wide open, but I noticed a cargo floater moving toward the same ramp, so I jogged over, trying to keep the floater between me and the ramp.

As I neared the cargo floater sliding down the ramp, something tripped me up and I sprawled into the dirt. As I rolled over, I found Jewels standing over me. "Stop lying around and follow me," she hissed, then hurried away.

I pushed myself up and trotted after her. We crossed the cargo dock and went down an alley lined with trash cans. Rick poked his head out from behind a can as we approached, and asked, "What are you doing here?"

"I could ask you two the same question. I followed a courier from The Caverns and he went down into the cargo landing."

"Well, we just came with a shipment of potions from the docks. They all went in there," Rick pointed.

"Why are the potions coming into the Triangle?" I asked.

Neither Jewels nor Rick had an answer for me, not that I expected one. I stood, chewing my mustache for a few breaths, then set off toward the main entrance to the arena.

"Wait! Where are you going?" Jewels hissed after me.

"We're in the middle of Tricrosse season," I replied. "One of the local teams is probably practicing right now, and I know an equipment manager for one of those teams. If I'm lucky, his team is in there right now and I can talk with him. He'll be straight with me."

Or so I hoped.

None of the main doors were opened, so I set off around the arena until I found a door marked "Players and Team Personnel Only" and tried it. It was unlocked and I stepped in and was immediately confronted by an armed ogre.

"No unauthorized people!" He barked.

"I'm here to see Eddie Markham. He wants to look at some of the gear I sell."

"Uh huh. Where's the gear, bub?"

"I've got a psydisc with all the details. Stuff's too heavy to carry around, right?" At least he hadn't said Eddie wasn't there.

The ogre eyed me from his statuesque height, but

apparently wasn't that big on trying to eject me. "Yeah, alright. Eddie's out in the stands watchin' practice." He motioned me on through a second door into a long hall. Doors along the hall announced locker rooms, team offices, equipment rooms, and the like until the hall emptied into a cavernous opening leading out onto the field.

I moved off to the side and climbed into the stands and shaded my eyes to look around. There were a bunch of players and coaches out on the field, working at various drills. A small clump of people was sitting a few sections away from me, near the field, watching the practice. One of them looked like Eddie.

I headed in their direction and they began staring at me. I could see some of them whispering among themselves, but then the guy who looked like Eddie stood up and came toward me.

"Betty!" Eddie greeted me. "What are you doing here, and how did you get in?"

"I came to talk to you, Eddie." I shifted to a whisper, "I told the door guard I was here to sell you some gear."

Eddie stared at me, then turned to the group. "A buddy I invited to come see the practice. He's clean!" He waved at them and they lost interest.

Eddie motioned for me to sit with him a little distance away. "What's really going on, Betty? I don't mind covering for you, but why would you barge in here just to chat with me?"

"It's about potions, Eddie."

He started. He didn't immediately deny knowing anything, just turned to look at the group he had been sitting with and then stared out over the field.

"How did you find out," he finally replied, speaking in a low tone just above a whisper.

I matched his volume as I gave a brief summary of the search that had led me to the Triangle. "What's going on, Eddie? Why are these super-strength potions being delivered here?"

Eddie was silent for a long time. When he spoke it was slowly and sadly. "You see the big guy out there, wearing the 52 jersey?" I looked out and saw a huge man working on some type of drill involving running—more like skipping—through rings placed on the ground. The guy was only a half-length or so taller than me, but must have weighed at least half again as much, and it was all muscle. He was bulging everywhere. I turned to Eddie and nodded.

"It's an open secret that pro players enhance," Eddie began. "Nobody wants to talk about it because everybody does it. It's how they compete. The

Tricrosse Commission says everyone's clean, but you can tell just by looking at players like Amra there that it ain't true. Nobody gets that kind of body built up and still stays fast and nimble on their feet through good diet and exercise. And once a few guys start enhancing, others start just to keep up.

"Yeah, there are a few who really are clean, but they don't get paid the big marks like Amra." Eddie turned to look me in the face. "You know he clears over a million a year, right?" I nodded. I followed the sport enough to have some inkling of the kinds of contracts the top players got.

"A few years ago, Amra's wife and coach tried to get him clean. They put him in a purge clinic and they took away his juice. Within days he couldn't get out of bed. His legs were too weak to hold his body upright. His spine couldn't move the weight of his torso. He was stuck lyin' in a bed getting somebody to spoon him food and clean him up after he messed himself 'cause he couldn't get to the bathroom. It was pitiful."

Eddie sighed. "The team's owner fired the coach and sent me to get Amra out of the clinic. We went in with a medical order and wheeled him out. Took five bottles of juice just for him to get off the stretcher and stumble into the floater. These guys aren't small-timers, Betty. They chug down so much juice it would kill a normal person."

"That's exactly what's been happening," I interrupted. "People are dying from super-strong potions. And we traced those potions here."

Eddie stared at me, wide-eyed. "Nobody's supposed to get the good stuff except the players. A year or so ago, the owner came up with the idea of getting extra strength potions so the guys wouldn't have to take a lot. Supposed to keep rumors of excessive use out of the psycasts. Nobody cares if players chug a bottle or two, but they didn't know those bottles were the same strength as half-a-dozen normal doses. What's going on out there?"

"Who manages the potions for the players?" I asked.

"Um, that would be me," Eddie admitted. He stared at the ground and his cheeks had turned red.

"You and me, we're going down to your equipment room and take a look at your inventory." I glared at Eddie. "Either someone's been stealing from you, or you and I are going to have a long talk about your side business."

Eddie stood up. "Yeah, I don't think so, Betty. I don't know what you're after, but you're going to have to bring a lawyer with you if you want me to cooperate. I got a good job and I ain't throwing it away to help you out. I like you, Betty, but not that much. I'm going back over with the other managers, and you can leave."

I hadn't seen him signal anything, so I assumed he had some kind of 'pathic link to the security guard, because he was coming out of the tunnel and heading straight for us. I stood up as well.

"It's been nice knowing you, Eddie. I'm sorry you don't want to help, but however the 'good stuff' is getting out to the public, I'm going to put a stop to it." I turned and strode right past the ogre guard, who followed me down the tunnel and out the side door.

TWELVE

I headed back around the arena, looking for the garbage platform where Rick and Jewels were waiting for me. I was too mad to think clearly. Eddie might not know the full extent of what was happening to his "good stuff," but he knew enough. We had the locus of the supply and distribution chains, now we had to start climbing it. I found Rick and Jewels right where I had left them and motioned them to follow me. Sam and Lilah were supposed to wait at Sam's place for us, so we found a cab and headed for the ogre side of town.

We found Sam and Lilah at Sam's apartment, and I filled everyone in on the conversation with Eddie at the arena. Sam was relaxing in an overstuffed chair. His eyes were closed, but a methodical tapping of his fingers on the arm of the chair suggested his mind was actively processing my story.

"The owners of Tricrosse teams are quite wealthy,"

he said as I finished. "But even a very wealthy man will feel the pinch of salaries, equipment purchases, and, apparently, funding potion addictions of the vast majority of the team. It would not surprise me if the extra potions were being sold at the owner's directive as a way of enhancing revenue."

"The team owners are usually also corp bigwigs," I added. "So what you're suggesting is one of the most powerful people in Fisk is also a potions dealer."

Sam nodded.

"But why?" asked Jewels. "Why buy extra and then sell it off? Are they that desperate for money?"

Sam held up a hand with one finger raised. "Two reasons. First, while they are, indeed, rich, wealthy people are rarely satisfied with what they have, and they want their business to appear profitable. Purchasing extra potions and selling them enhances their bottom line. Second, if news of the extra-strength potion use by players ever leaks to the public, they can dissemble and say their players are getting the potions from the same market as the public. Thus, their credibility is protected and a player or two will be sacrificed in the name of 'doing something' about the problem. The public will move on to other 'problems' and the juicing by players will be forgotten."

"That's quite a conspiracy theory you're cooking

up, Sam," Jewels scoffed.

"No, he's right," Lilah spoke up. "It's not a conspiracy, it's just the way big business owners think. The most important thing is to protect money flow, and money flow is dependent on reputation at least as much as actual profitability. I would think especially in this case, where the main product is entertainment. If people lose trust in the integrity of the team, they will abandon them."

"This is all very interesting," I interrupted, "but how do we get these potions off the street?"

No one said anything for a few moments, then Sam spoke up. "Allow me to summarize what we know. First, we cannot attack the producers because there are too many clans in Durgaland providing these potions. Second, we cannot attack the distributor, because it is coming from a corp, one of the most powerful organizations in Fisk. Whcrc docs that leave us?"

"The supply chain," I answered. "We have to disrupt the flow of potions." I heaved a sigh. "Still not an easy job. And which supply chain do we go after? The potions coming into port, or the ones going out to the public?"

"The chain to the public is smaller," Sam stated.

"I just don't know," I said, "the chain is smaller, but how do you break it up? Take out a few runners and dealers and more will pop up. We could be chasing this snake for the rest of our lives and not have an effect."

"You people aren't very bright, are you?"

We all turned to stare at Rick. "Well?" he said. "Supply lines are easily replaceable. The corp is too big. The only way to do this is go after the Durgahh making the potions."

"I thought you said there were too many tribes making potions," I reminded him.

"I did, when I thought it was you and me. But now that my daughter and this gifted little elf," (Jewels bristled at the 'little' appellation, and I waved her down while Rick continued without noticing), "are with us, I have an idea." He chuckled and rubbed his hands together, "A truly delightful idea."

"Well," Lilah said, "spit it out, Dad."

He chuckled again, "We ruin the supply."

"What? How?" I spit out.

"We'll set up shop in Banjall. Lilahh, Jewels, and I will make joke potions. You and your ogre friend will have to sneak into the warehouses and replace the special potions with ours. As the joke potions work their way into circulation, it will start a war between the corp and the clans."

"Something about this doesn't seem quite right," I started.

"I think it might be our only way," Sam interrupted. "Though I will have to refrain from the 'sneaking into warehouses' part. I am not built for that. I will stay as protection for you three and Betty will have to handle the swapping of potions."

"I can't replace enough potions by myself in one night to make a difference," I protested.

Rick answered me, "You don't have to replace a lot each time. Besides, the three of us won't be able to produce more than about a dozen each day. It will take a half-month or more, but the cumulative effect of multiple joke potions showing up in multiple supply chains will get the corps' notice."

"And that's when the fun starts?" I asked.

"Yeah," Rick answered, and chuckled again.

Thirteen

I shuffled along the street, a bag of potion bottles slung over my back. Each bottle was wrapped in cloth to keep them from breaking, and from clanking. Over nearly a month, I had learned the best way to avoid being noticed in a city full of trolls was to keep my head down, my eyes glued to the street in front of me, and to plod wearily. Looking up and striding were perceived by the trolls as an expression of superiority and a direct challenge.

I trudged into the warehouse district and went into the alleys between the big buildings. The warehouses in Banjall were all built back-to-back, with parallel streets running along the fronts. This left narrow alleys between the backs of the buildings as well as along each side. Most of the warehouses had a door out the back for disposing of garbage into the alleys, which made them perfect for pilfering jobs.

The first night I had tried to infiltrate a warehouse,

I didn't start out until after dark. That turned out to be a mistake as a human wandering around Banjall at night was too suspicious to the trolls. They followed me around everywhere and I had to abandon the mission. So I spent a day scouting the area and found a good hiding spot on top of a warehouse. This particular building was lower than the others and had a ladder built into the outside wall. I had no idea what the purpose of getting on the roof was, but I took advantage of it. Looking along the alley, I made sure no one was around, then scurried up the ladder and lay down on the roof, setting my bag gently beside me.

I would wait until an hour or so after sunset, and then find my mark for the evening. Originally, we wanted to spread our joke potions around, but Sam reasonably pointed out that these shipments could be going to Tricrosse teams or other outlets all over Ilanerra and spreading the adulterated ones out that far would not have the effect we wanted. We had to focus only on the potions going to Fisk and try to only replace the extra-strength potions. Replacing a run-of-the-mill enhancing potion wouldn't be enough of an issue to bring the corps' wrath to Durgaland.

It took Sam and Rick together several days to figure out which warehouses were being used by the clans supplying Fisk. While they worked, Lilah and Jewels concocted a way for me to "see" inside the crates and detect the strength of the spells emanating from the contents. They tried to explain it to me, but I lost them somewhere around "natural shift anomalies." I just trusted the bracelet they came up with, which caused the extra-strength potions inside crates to pulse with a green glow that seeped out of the cracks in the packing materials.

I lay on the roof, trying to stay relaxed without falling asleep. The sun had been a little above the horizon when I lay down and was now painting the sky a dirty orange. I estimated I had about two hours before I could get started. I heard movement and low voices in the alley below me, which was a little out of the ordinary for so late in the day. I tried to catch what they were saying, then realized they were speaking troll, so it would do no good to listen in.

The voices stopped right below me and then I heard the worst sound possible. Someone was coming up the ladder. I panicked for an instant, and then pulled out my nature wand and dissolved the wood around the metal clasps at the top of the ladder. The whole thing gave way and fell backwards. Someone screamed and the ladder hit the wall on the opposite side of the alley and stuck there. A couple of different voices were yelling now, but they quieted quickly and I heard a thud as something hit the ground.

There was some muted conversation, then the

ladder lifted itself upright and I heard metal scraping across the paving stones as the ladder moved back toward me, but came in lower than the top edge. They were leaning it up against the building and were going to come up anyway. There was no way off this roof, and no way I was going to blindly cut through the roof and drop down, so it was going to be a fight. I slid over toward where the ladder had been, and lay flat on my back with my knees pulled up to my chin.

A troll poked his head over the edge of the roof, a little to the left of where I thought he should be. I lashed out with one foot and caught him with a glancing blow. It was enough to make him lose his hold and he screamed as he fell.

I quickly rolled over and stuck my head over the edge and that was almost the end of my mission. An ice bolt splattered only a span away from my head, and ice shards stung my cheek. I pulled back and put my hand to my face and felt blood. I was lucky I hadn't lost an eye. It was time to get out of here.

There were four small glass pyramids set into the roof of this particular warehouse, but I had never been curious enough to look through them. I listened for a moment, but heard no more movement up the ladder. Whoever was down there was probably calling for reinforcements and I had very little time to make decisions.

Looking through the glass of one of the pyramids, I saw a fairly standard warehouse below me, with stacks of crates and racks of shelves laden with smaller boxes. There was nothing right below me, so I ran over to another pyramid and below this one was a stack of crates that looked close enough for me to drop onto and sturdy enough to hold me.

I had never tried my nature wand on glass before, and found it had no effect. I moved instead to the wooden frames holding the glass and had soon loosened one enough that it fell, shattering on the crates below with a loud crash. The sound brought renewed shouting from below, so I quickly dislodged another piece of glass, which gave me enough room to wiggle myself through.

My bag of bottles still lay where I had left them, and I stood for a moment deciding their fate. There was no way they were going to survive the night; the question was whether I could just abandon them. I grunted and shook my head as I realized that wasn't a choice, so I grabbed the bag and dropped it into the warehouse below. I heard some bottles shatter and almost wept for the loss of such a large amount of work.

I backed through the window, let myself down until I was hanging by my fingers, then dropped to the crates below. One foot came down on my bag and slipped out from under me, my other leg buckled and I landed painfully on my rear with my left leg bent back sharply. A sudden pang shot across my left thigh and I knew I had strained something. Grumbling with exasperation, I untangled myself, grabbed the bag, now sodden with the leaking potions, and clambered down from the pile of crates.

There was still enough light dripping through the windows on the roof to illuminate the warehouse, but it was going to be dark soon. The warehouse was typical of the type I had been sneaking into—a big box with large doors on the main street side and one smaller door on the alley side, and no windows, only the skylights for light.

I wasn't going out the alley door, and I didn't want to try the street doors right away either. There would still be traffic on the street and I would attract way too much attention. In one corner of the warehouse a room had been fashioned by putting up a couple of walls, and I decided I would hide in there.

My left leg was tender, and I limped a bit as I hurried across to the corner room. The door was locked, and I didn't want to carve out the lock with my nature wand as that would be too obvious to anyone searching the place. There was a stack of crates next to one wall, and I climbed them and found there was no top to the room, just the walls. Once again I dropped my bag of potions and then dropped near them. The room was some type of office, with a desk, a couple of chairs, and several cabinets.

I sat in the chair, drew my fire wand, and waited. My leg was throbbing, and I stretched and flexed it, trying to ease the pain. It was quite some time before I heard several voices outside. I didn't hear anyone climb the ladder, but I did hear footsteps on the roof. There was some shouting, then I heard the back door open.

Multiple footsteps entered the warehouse, echoing off the walls. They moved slowly. I knew they must be spreading out, searching the place. Eventually, someone tried the door and found it locked. I raised my wand in readiness as the searchers shouted at each other in troll.

"We know you're in here, skel!" The voice had a gravely rasp that made it a little hard to understand. The other trolls were continuing to move around the building, and I could hear them moving crates around.

"We just want to talk," the troll continued. "Come out and you won't get hurt."

I kept silent. "You won't get hurt" is one of the oldest lies in the world. Especially for hired thugs, like I used to be. Right outside the office, somebody was beginning to move the crates I had climbed to get in here. I shifted my weight and pointed my fire wand up toward the top of the wall. Whoever was moving the crates yelled and I soon heard gravel-voice muttering something outside, and then he yelled loudly in troll. The warehouse went silent, except for the sound of approaching footsteps.

"It's over, skel. There are a lot of us and one of you and you're surrounded. Come out. You're going with us, but we can carry you if we have to."

He wasn't threatening death, and specifically said they would carry me, which meant they were here to collect me, not kill me. I was slightly tempted to go with them just to find our who had sent them.

But only slightly.

I lowered my head to ponder the situation and that's when I noticed I was sitting on a trap door. In my pre-occupation with the hunters outside, I had never taken a thorough look at my surroundings. I shrugged, yelled, "Alright, give me a moment," and stood up and shoved the chair to the side. Under the desk was a rope attached to a loop in the trap door, so I stooped under, grabbed it and heaved the panel up.

A ladder led down into a dark shaft, but I could hear the sound of water lapping up against something below me. I let myself down and found myself in a tunnel, half filled with salt water. I needed a light of some kind, but didn't have one, so I carefully waded in the only open direction, running my hands along the side of the tunnel.

I began to feel slightly nauseated and tense. I didn't like being closed up in this space, but I grit my teeth and continued pushing ahead into darkness. I don't know how much time passed before I became aware of a gradual lightening of the gloom around me. My heart was racing by then and I picked up the pace, hurrying toward what I could now make out was a patch of gray in the overwhelming black around me.

The tunnel ended abruptly, and the ground dropped out from under my feet. I found myself treading water underneath one of the piers in the harbor. I swam out into open water and looked around until I spied a ladder climbing up to one of the docks. An hour later I finally dragged myself into our rented rooms, dripping wet, with a sore leg, and sore spirit.

Fourteen

The rest of my crew was asleep, so I crept as quietly as I could into the bedroom I shared with Rick, found some fresh clothes, and changed as quietly as I could before collapsing on my bed. Since everyone assumed I had been working all night, I was allowed to sleep late. Hunger woke me earlier than normal, and I limped out to the common room.

Finding any kind of rental in Banjall would have been difficult enough, as there were precious few apartments in the city, and only one small group of apartments near the docks had anything ogre-sized. As luck would have it, just as we made inquiries, an ogre apartment had come open and we were able to get a month-to-month contract on it. So, our rooms were quite comfortable for Sam, but the rest of us struggled with all the ogre-sized furniture and fixtures.

The dining table had become the de-facto workspace for Lilah, Rick, and Jewels, and they were all clustered on top of it with their bottles, minerals, and solutions. I had been able to watch them work the first few days as we searched for a place to distribute their product, but I still didn't understand the process very well.

They purchased large bags of ground minerals rich in metals, used some type of melding wand to infuse handfuls of powder with a spell, then dissolved the powder in a potable solution. I had tried one of their concoctions and it tasted nasty, but I found myself suddenly able to float a foot or so above the ground, which was exhilarating. I began to understand why some people got addicted to the stuff.

The three of them were there now, bent over their work, while Sam sat on a sofa by the window. He was the first to notice me and my limp.

"Rough night, Betty?"

"You could say that. I was ambushed at my hiding place."

I had everyone's attention now, so I settled into a chair and told the whole story. Lilah gasped several times as I talked, and immediately climbed down from the table and came over to check my leg and face. Rick and Sam actually seemed pleased, grinning broadly at each other.

"What are you two grinning about? Ow!" I reacted as Lilah pressed on the side of my knee. "Are you a doctor?"

"No," she replied, "I'm just checking to see where it hurts."

"Well, I already know where it hurts so please quit poking at my leg."

Lilah jerked back, an offended look on her face.

"Take it easy, skel," Rick's growl cut over Lilah's attempted rejoinder. "She's just trying to help."

"I'm sorry," I sighed. "I had a rough night. My leg is sore but usable—probably just pulled a muscle and I almost took an ice spike in the eye. But mostly I'm irritated that I was seen and tracked. I didn't mean to take it out on you." Lilah headed back to the table, her stiff back showing she wasn't entirely mollified.

"But, do you not see, Betty," Sam interjected. "This is exactly what we have been waiting for. Someone, either a Durgahh clan or a corp, is reacting to our pollution of the supply." He paused for a moment. "You probably should have let yourself be taken, so we could find out who is after us."

"Oh, that would have been brilliant, with no way of contacting you to come get me."

Sam turned to the three on the table, "Lilah, how far away can you sense Betty's thoughts?"

Lilah stared down at the table for a moment before answering, "If I concentrate, I could probably pick him up from across the Durgahh Straights."

I was stunned. "You can hear me from that distance? I thought mind techs had to be within a few blocks, at most, of their target?"

"After we linked minds last year, I've been able to pick up your thoughts almost whenever I want." Lilah mumbled.

Rick, Jewels, and I stared at Lilah, but Sam rubbed his hands together. "That is perfect. You go back out tonight and let yourself be taken, then Lilah tracks you to wherever they take you and we rescue you, after you discover who is behind the attack."

"No, Sam," I replied. "First, they could easily put a mental block on me. Second, I thought what we wanted was a war between the clans and the corps. Letting someone interrogate me would negate that."

Sam checked off my objections on his fingers, "First, most interrogation techniques involve trying to read the subject's mind. They would have to unblock you for such an attempt. Second, what better way to start a war than to identify yourself as working for the other side?"

I stared at Sam as Rick chuckled. "He's right. This is a golden opportunity. You can't pass it up."

"Oh, yes. Yes, I can. I don't really want to be dragged off who knows where and 'interrogated.' That's happened to me before and I didn't enjoy it."

"He's right," Lilah added. "We can't risk him

breaking under pressure and revealing us and our entire plan."

I appreciated her support, yet was also a little offended. "You think I'd break?"

"Yeah," Jewels finally spoke up. "If Betty tells them what we've been up to, the cats and the corps all come after us. This is not a good idea."

"Now hold up there you two. Sam's idea would work, I'm just not happy with being bait."

"Well, it's for the best," Lilah said. "I hate to think how they might poke you where it hurts."

I glared at her. I probably deserved it, but I was mad anyway. I looked at Sam. "Alright, I'll do it. But I want all of you close by, in case the 'capture' goes bad."

Sam rubbed his hands together. "Fantastic. I rather think we should wait a night or two before you go back, so as not to arouse suspicion. That will give us plenty of time to plan this out."

"Good," I said, "then I'll go back to bed and rest my sore leg." I limped off back to my room. It only occurred to me much later that I had been manipulated into agreeing to this insanity.

Two days later I was weaving my way through the alleys behind the warehouses, making for my usual spot. I had a bag slung over my shoulder, filled with joke potions. We wanted the "product" I had been distributing available for inspection. I finally reached my destination and found the first problem—the ladder was gone. I had broken it the last time I was here, and it hadn't been repaired. It wasn't even just propped up against the building any more, it was just gone.

I sighed. I was going to have to find another hiding place, but that wouldn't help me get captured unless they had followed me here. I hadn't been trying to escape notice because I wanted to be noticed. I just hadn't seen anyone following me. I turned around and found the alley blocked by trolls with wands. Looked like the plan's first stage was going to work just fine.

A Note From Betty

To my readers: I know you've become accustomed to me telling the story, but the next several days were, from my point of view, not very interesting. I suppose you would like to know the details of how they "asked" me questions, but...well, it's not really all that entertaining, and something I'd rather forget, anyway.

The point is, what you really need to know is how Lilah, Sam, Jewels, and Rick tracked me down and rescued me. What follows is what I've been able to piece together from the four of them. It's probably not completely accurate, but, unlike me, none of them keep a daily journal so I was relying solely on their memories.

Oh, and they insisted I spell their names correctly. I guess I really need to learn these troll names, even if I can't pronounce them.

FIFTEEN

"You lost him?"

"Yes, Jewels," Lilahh answered. "We knew they would probably shield him. We have to wait for him to become visible again. They'll have to take his shield off when they interrogate him."

"Are you sure you'll be able to figure out his location?"

"We went through all this, remember?" Lilahh was getting a little exasperated. "It will take a while, but I can sense the general direction he's in and we'll just work our way toward him by...what did you call it, Sam?"

"Triangulation."

"Yeah. That."

"I'm really nervous about this."

"We already talked this out, elf," Rikk said.

"My name's not "elf"!"

"And mine's not "cat."" The two glared at each

other.

"Clearly," Sam began, "the tension is wearing on all of us. Until such time as Betty's thoughts become visible to Lilahh, we can do nothing but wait. Perhaps it would be best if we did not all wait together in the same room."

Jewels and Rikk each stomped off to their rooms, leaving Sam and Lilahh alone in the main room.

"Do you really think we did the right thing, Sam?"

"We are doing our best, using the information known to us, and that is always the 'right' thing to do. I understand your concern for Betty, but he has been through worse."

"What exactly did Betty do before signing up with Joshua. He's always really vague when I ask him."

"It is not my place to tell Betty's story, but he used to work as a freelance enforcer for the corps. When someone 'got out of line,' as they say, Betty would be dispatched to beat them into submission."

"He was a bull?"

"Um, yes, I believe that is the colloquial term for his work,"

Lilahh sat silent for a while. "I never really figured *that* out," she finally said. "He always said he did 'work' for the corps, and I could hear the quotes around 'work.' I should have known..."

"You did not see this when you mind-linked with

him?"

"Well, I was kind of focused only on the one incident. I've spent most of my life learning to weed out extraneous information. If I couldn't do that, I'd go insane from the miscellaneous thoughts being shouted all around me."

She was silent again, then heaved a big sigh. "I got worked over by bulls a couple of times while I was rising up through the ranks in the hold." Another pause. "And then I hired bulls to do 'work' a few times while I was Director. It's just the way we did things, but still..."

"You asked if we were doing right. There are times when doing the right thing is to avoid doing the wrong thing."

"Didn't you used to work with him?"

"In a manner of speaking. I avoided working with the corps by focusing on my music and performance. But, I did need extra money on occasion, and Betty would offer me jobs where we needed to discover who was exploiting their corp-provided job. Once the perpetrator was found, my part would be finished. And, yes, before you ask, I am guilty by association."

"Why do we put up with it, Sam?"

"It is the way of the world, Lilahh. And who is going to go to war with the corps?"

"Isn't that what we're doing right now?"

"I suppose it is."

"I think we need to help change the world, Sam. Maybe that's why Betty is so eager about doing these jobs for Joshua. He's making up for his past."

"I cannot speak toward his motivation, but I think we may have all found the right path."

Lilahh gave a little smile to Sam, then gasped. "There he is!" She closed her eyes and concentrated. "Sort of that way," she said, pointing off to her left.

Sam grabbed a compass and sighted along Lilahh's arm. "East by northeast. Can you estimate distance?"

"He's not terribly far away. Maybe still in the city."

"Then we wait."

"What!?"

"It is too early to chase after him. Our goal is to initiate conflict between the corps and their Durgahh suppliers. That mission is not accomplished by rescuing Betty prior to his interrogation, when, hopefully, he can pass false information to his abductors. We must wait until he is higher up the food chain, as the expression goes."

"But, can't we...he's gone." Lilahh heaved a big sigh. "I think this plan might be harder on me than it is on Betty."

"We at least know which direction they are headed. It is possible they will stay here in Banjall rather than take him to a clan demesne, which will facilitate our speed in rescuing him when the time comes."

"That doesn't make me feel a lot better."

"Perhaps you should get some sleep. It is rather late, and tomorrow we will need you at your best in order to track him."

"I know you're right, but I can't sleep right now."

"As you think best. I am going to retire." Sam paused and laid a hand on Lilahh's arm. "I understand your concern. Get some rest, it is the best thing you can do for Betty right now."

Lilahh gave Sam a wan smile, and the ogre got up and went to his room. She stayed nestled on the couch, listening in vain for some hint of Betty's presence, and that's where Jewels found her, fast asleep, in the morning.

Jewels shook the sleeping troll, "Get up, sleepyhead. We need you listening for Betty."

"Ugh. What time is it?"

"Two hours past sunrise. At least. Get up." Jewels shook Lilahh again.

"Stop. I'm awake. Just give me a chance to stretch. This isn't a comfortable bed."

"What are you doing out here, anyway?"

"I think I fell asleep while listening. I should have climbed down and gone to bed, but I was too focused on Betty."

"Well, that's what you're supposed to be doing, so I

guess that's OK." Jewels floated off toward the kitchen in search of food.

Lilahh stayed on the ogre-sized couch, working out the kinks in her neck and legs. Rikk shambled out, grunted a greeting to Lilahh and headed for the kitchen. A few moments later, Sam came in through the front door. As usual, he had risen earlier than everyone else and gone out for a morning walk.

"Good morning," he greeted them. The other three just glared at him.

"Well, such a happy team this morning! So you will be pleased to know our stratagem is having the desired effect. A DQI yacht is in the harbor!" Sam rubbed his hands together gleefully.

"Are you sure?" Lilahh gasped. "What would they be doing...Oh."

"Yes!" Sam chuckled.

"What? What are you talking about?" Rikk was querulous.

"DQI is one of the big corps," Jewels piped in. "Maybe the biggest. Their execs hardly ever leave their palaces. They wouldn't come here unless something big was happening."

"Betty," Rikk stated.

"Of course," Sam said, "they are here to 'interview' Betty. I smell an opportunity."

"What are you cooking up, Sam?" Jewels was

suspicious.

"We strike first!" Sam exclaimed. "Instead of waiting for them to take us to Betty, we invade their yacht and kidnap an exec. Then we can negotiate Betty's release and a cessation of the potion trade."

Jewels groaned. "I was afraid you were going to say something like that."

Sixteen

"This is nuts."

"You have said that multiple times, Jewels."

"That's because it's nuts, Sam! We're sitting right next to a yacht with more tech than I've seen in my life. There's so many shields around that thing right now I wouldn't believe it was there if I wasn't looking at it."

"Do those shields go all around the ship?"

"Of course they do! You think I'm an idiot?"

"Have you probed under the water?"

"Yes!...Well, actually, no, I think I might have stopped at the water line."

"Why don't you check now?"

Jewels' eyes unfocused as she probed toward the large ship on the other side of the docks. "Well, I'll be a neutral. The only shield under the boat is a force shield to stop physical attacks."

"Naturally." Sam sounded smug.

"Spit it out, Sam. How did you know?"

"It is standard practice for ogre shipping. They use a variety of sensors to probe the water to detect depth and underwater threats, such as reefs. Shields would affect their ability, so they only use psychic and spell shields above the waterline. The force shields protect the hull and help prevent leaks, but they will not stop your ability to affect the metal with various spells."

"So I burn a hole in the bottom of their boat? Won't it sink?"

"Not only will your ability to superheat the metal be impacted by the surrounding water, but it will take a long time to melt the metal away and that will give the crew time to react to our incursion. I would suggest freezing a patch of metal. We can then easily break through it despite the force shield, which will prevent the boat from sinking."

"So we wait until the cats have the corp bigwig down in the hold, then we break the boat and all swim back here to our little shed."

"Boathouse, Jewels."

"Looks to me like a shed without a floor."

Sam ignored her. "Here come Lilahh and Rikk."

The two trolls, wearing Treoynn vests, were shuffling along the dock, pushing crates on floater carts. When they reached the yacht's berth, Rikk yelled for attention. A bored-looking guard walked over to the nearest railing and yelled back, "What do you want?"

Rikk yelled something in troll. "I don't growl, cat. If you want something, speak like a person."

Lilahh spoke up using a heavy accent, "We are sorry for disturb you. We have supplies for boat."

"What supplies?"

"I am sorry," Lilahh kept up her act. "We carry supplies from clan for boat. We are not told what in boxes."

"Hey, Frank! Come over here, will ya."

Another guard ambled over. "What's going on, Harvey?"

"I got a couple cats down on the dock sayin' they're delivering somethin' from a clan."

The second guard stared down at Rikk and Lilahh. "They prob'ly got some juice for the bosses. They're just a couple of trolls and they're wearing the right mark. Check the crates, then let 'em in and take 'em up to VIP to drop off the goods. Then send 'em right back off the boat. Nothin' else and keep your wand on 'em."

"Alright, Frank, if you say so." Harvey yelled down to the trolls, "Stay there and wait for the gangplank. We'll let you on, but no funny business. You drop the crates and then you leave. Understand?"

"Yes, sir, we do as you say," Lilahh replied.

Both guards disappeared and several moments

passed before a hatch lower on the boat opened and a passerelle extended out to the dock. Sam and Jewels could see Harvey standing just inside the hatch, his wand pointing at Rikk and Lilahh as they pushed their carts over into the yacht. At the hatch opening, Harvey pried open a crate and looked inside. He appeared satisfied and led the two into the yacht.

Across the pier in the boathouse, Jewels laughed. "One good thing about Betty rummaging around warehouses is we got a nice supply of potions to box up and send over to our friends."

"Indeed," Sam agreed. "Now, we should give Lilahh and Rikk about a quarter hour to execute their part of the plan, then we head into the water and open the hull."

"I sure hope this works," Jewels said.

"As do I." Sam said. "As do I."

***

Inside the boat, Lilahh and Rikk trudged along behind the guard as they passed through a tender garage to a narrow, circular stairway. The guard turned to them, "You'll have to carry them up from here. You ain't gettin' those floaters up the st—" He cut off suddenly as his eyes rolled up in his head and he slumped onto the stairs.

"Quick," whispered Rikk. "Pull him out of sight."

The two dragged the guard to the nearest tender

and heaved him up into the small boat. "Why'd you have to knock him out so early?" Rikk grunted as they heaved the guard over the gunwale.

"Because no one was nearby right now and we won't have a better chance later. Let's combine the crates and take the empty one upstairs."

"Are you sure you know where you're going on this boat?" Rikk opened up both crates and lifted out the racks of potions sitting in the top of each crate. Underneath was nothing but a frame to hold the racks up, giving the illusion of full crates.

"Yes, Daddy. I've been to enough parties on corp yachts. They all have the same basic layout. The executive saloon will be forward on the main deck. If there aren't any bosses hanging out in the saloon, their quarters are one deck down from the saloon."

Lilahh removed the frame from one crate and put both racks into that crate and shoved it and the frames against the wall of the garage. She and Rikk picked up the now empty crate and carried it up the stairs to reach the main deck. Crew and guests were moving around up here, but gave little more than a glance at two trolls carrying a box.

The two Durgahh worked their way forward toward the grand saloon, a palatial room with sweeping vistas of the water that now looked out on the dull gray stone of the wharf and warehouses that made up the docks district. A small group of finely dressed people glanced up as they entered, then returned to their conversations. A burly guard blocked their way into the saloon.

"Whatcha doin' 'ere?" He growled.

Lilahh kept up the servile troll act, "We bring goods from Treoynn Clan for big boss."

The guard grunted. "'Big boss is busy. You come wif me and drop 'at in 'er cabin." The guard herded Lilahh and Rikk back into the passageway and then squeezed past them and headed toward a stairwell.

They followed the guard down into a passageway lined by dark-stained wood doors. As they headed down the hall, Lilahh stumbled and dropped her end of the crate, hissing as she did so.

"'ey! Watch yerself, cat!" The guard yelled. Lilahh grabbed her end of the crate and lifted, shaking her head at her father's questioning look.

The Durgahh continued after the guard and he ushered them into a cabin that opened at the end of the passageway. The room was spacious and opulent, presided over by an impossibly huge bed raised on a pedestal under a mirrored ceiling.

"Unload the juice over 'ere," the guard pointed to a cabinet on the port side of the cabin. Lilahh and Rikk wrestled the crate over near the cabinet and pulled off the top, then just stared into the empty box. "What's 'at you got?" The guard pulled a wand and strode over and stared into the crate. "Where's the jui..." He got no further as Rikk ripped off his cap and Lilahh focused on him and put him to sleep.

"Ugh. He's heavy," Lilahh grunted as she and Rikk pulled the guard out of the crate into which he had partially fallen.

"What happened outside?" Rikk asked. "Did you just trip?"

"No, it's Betty! He's in one of those other cabins. I suddenly sensed him as we walked past. They must have the cabin shielded, but they got sloppy and let the shield extend into the hall. We walked past the door and there he was!"

"Well, well, well. What do you want to bet the 'big boss' is in there questioning him?"

"So what? We can get Betty out and then we don't need the exec as a bargaining chip."

"Play the long game, girl. We need to know what's going on. We take the exec and we get answers."

"Alright, dad. And don't call me girl."

"I'm your father and you're my girl, don't fuss. Let's go. Leave the crate."

The two Durgahh peered out into the passageway to verify it was empty, then hurried down the hall until Lilahh sensed Betty. She moved close to either door, and then settled on the port side cabin. "He's in here," she whispered.

"You're inside their shield, can you tell who's in there?"

"Betty and two others. I don't want to probe too hard in case one of the other two is sensitive."

Rikk ran his hands over the door. "This is genuine wood. I can turn it into dust in a few seconds. Then what?"

"Well, I can sense the other two, so they're not personally shielded. I can knock them out."

"OK. Ready?" Rikk asked. Lilahh nodded. Rikk nodded back and placed his hands on the door, which suddenly opened, revealing a guard with wand pointed straight at the two Durgahh.

SEVENTEEN

Some twenty lengths away from the startled Durgahh, Jewels carefully felt along the hull, near the stern of the boat, searching for the echo of a large hold space beyond. Sam floated nearby, his features fuzzy from the physical shield Jewels had formed around his head.

"Please move quickly, Jewels, I cannot breathe inside this shield quite as long as you."

"I'm hurryin', I'm hurryin'." Jewels clipped off her words in exasperation as she continued to feel along the hull. "Oh! I think I found it." The elf backed off a bit from the hull and aimed a constant stream of ice directly at the metal. Chunks of ice drifted out from her body as water around her froze and broke away.

"I think that is enough," Sam panted. Jewels backed up and Sam began gently pounding on the affected area. After a few strikes, bits of metal began disintegrating and floating off into the water. Sam kept tapping and the hole widened.

"Why aren't the shields stopping this?" Jewels asked.

"The shields are on the inside," Sam replied. "They cannot be outside the hull without ruining the buoyancy of the ship. The hull can be breached, but the shields will not let anything, including water, into the ship. The shields are one-way so workers inside the ship can reach through them to patch the breach. When Lilahh and Rikk arrive, they will be able to exit. There, this will be large enough. I need air." Sam quickly rose toward the surface, Jewels floating up after him.

As they broke the surface, Jewels dropped the shields around their heads and Sam gulped in large quantities of fresh air. After several breaths, Sam nodded and Jewels set the shields up again and the two dove beneath the water and swam back toward the boathouse.

Sam scrambled up the ladder, heaving himself onto the dock, while Jewels levitated over to the door and peered through.

"Looks normal," she said.

Sam came up beside her and cracked the door wider so he could get a good view of the yacht. "We appear to have avoided notice. Now we wait until we hear from Lilahh and then I create a diversion..."

"And I help the cats get out of the bag!" Jewels cackled at her own joke.

Sam rolled his eyes and then went back to watching the boat.

***

Hi, it's Betty. I'm taking over from here...

***

A soft, lilting voice spoke from behind the guard. "We've been watching you since you came aboard. Won't you join us?"

The guard retreated, wand held ready, and Lilahh and Rikk stepped into the cabin, which was set up as a conference room with a large table and a dozen or more chairs. Lilahh gasped when she saw me tied up in one of those chairs and she tried to run over to me, but the guard prodded her with his wand and she backed up, face twisting in a snarl.

"Ease up, Lilah, I'm okay," I assured her. "We don't need to start a fight. Yet."

She relaxed a bit and looked around, her face registering surprise at the sight of the other troll woman sitting across from me.

"Lilah, meet Jaydah. She's the Executive Vice-President for Customer Relations..." I paused. "Did I get that right?" The troll nodded. "...Customer Relations for DQI. She's been asking me questions about the fakes. I've been telling her stories about my childhood."

"Your boyfriend here is quite adept at avoiding answering any questions, even with my telepath sitting here," Jaydahh nodded at the other person in the room, a shabby, old man who seemed half asleep.

"He's not my boyfriend," Lilahh said.

"I don't care. All I care about is getting answers and now that you two are here, and, I assume, in league with him," Jaydahh jerked her head toward me, "we'll try one of you."

"You won't get anything out of her," the old man said, rousing himself enough to sit up a little. "She's a stronger 'path than I am. And you probably can't get anything out of the other troll either, but he's her father, so threatening him..."

Jaydahh's eyes lit up. "Yes, I like that very much. Get two more guards down here." The old man's head sunk back into his chest and his eyes drooped as he reached out and ordered two men to come to the cabin.

"Get those two to sit down next to their friend," Jaydahh ordered the guard in the room. The man wordlessly waved Lilahh and Rikk to get chairs and move them next to me. Rikk slid a chair over near me and patted my arm, which was strapped down to the arm of the chair.

"Got my boy tied up right tight now, don't ya?" He

asked. As he patted my arm, I felt the ropes loosen and looked down. He had dissolved them. So much for natural fiber ropes. I didn't wait to see if the thug would notice. I leaped to my feet and swung my other arm, still attached to the chair, and slammed said seat into the guard's face. He dropped, Jaydah shouted and alarms began ringing all over the boat.

Lilahh grabbed a piece of the broken chair and clubbed the now well-awake telepath who was struggling to stand. His eyes rolled up in his head and he fell back into his chair. "Too late to stop the alarm, but he won't communicate with anyone."

"Thanks," I said. "What was the rescue plan?"

"Not a rescue," Rikk said. "Kidnapping. We were coming for someone like her," he pointed at Jaydahh, who still sat bemused by all the activity. "We figured we take an exec from the corp and then do a trade."

"OK," I said, "well, now it can bc both. Wc all gct out of here and take her with us. Something big's happening and she'll tell us what we need to know."

"I'm not going with you, Mr. Sterling, because you aren't going anywhere. This ship is now locked down tighter than my personal vault. You won't get out."

I looked at Lilahh and Rikk.

"Sam and Jewels knocked a hole in the bottom of the boat. We swim out and Jewels comes and gives us shields to let us swim underwater. No one sees us get away."

I grabbed the guard's wand and the exec's arm and said, "Sounds good, let's go."

"Let go of me!" Jaydahh shouted, struggling against my grip, then she slumped.

"It's easier this way," Lilahh said.

"Yeah, but now I have to carry her," I whined.

"You're a big, strong man. You can do it."

I snorted, then hefted the troll over my shoulder. I held her in place with one hand and held the guard's wand in the other. "Let's go."

That was when the two summoned guards burst into the room. I instinctively fired the wand just as Rikk bowled into the leading guard, slamming him backwards into his companion. The wand was a lightning wand, and the bolt that struck the guard sent sparks flying. The guard I hit dropped to the floor and lay jerking, as if in a macabre dance. Both Rikk and the other guard skipped backward, and I could smell burnt fur and knew Rikk had taken some of the brunt of the attack.

I caught the second guard with another blast and he flew through the doorway as I pushed into Rikk to get him moving. "Go go go go go," I urged him.

Rikk went swiftly out into the hall and turned toward the stern. I motioned Lilah out after him, and followed, walking half-backward so I could see anyone coming after us. Rikk led us into a master cabin where another guard lay on the floor next to a large, empty crate.

"Why did you bring us back here, Dad?"

Rikk pointed. "When we came in here earlier, I noticed those doors that open outside. Some kind of private veranda. Faster than trying to find our way back to the hold, and no stairways crawling with guards."

"How do we open it?" I asked.

"Probably that crank right there."

"Well, get cranking."

"I can't. You burned my hands."

Lilahh shouted in exasperation, "Men!" She ran over and started turning the winch to the right, but it stuck and wouldn't move.

"Other way, honey," Rikk said.

"Thanks. Dad." Lilahh said between clenched teeth as she struggled to turn it to the left. I dropped the troll exec and ran over and we both threw our weight into it and the side of the ship began lowering. It was about halfway down when shouting from the deck above was accompanied by a group of wand bursts of all types, shortly followed by pounding at the door.

"I'm out of ideas, folks," I said.

"I'll keep them out of the cabin," Rikk said. "You two get that door down." He stepped over to the door of the cabin and laid his hands on it. It began to grow, widening a little to more tightly fit into the frame, but mainly thickening, turning into a huge, immovable block of wood. Lilahh and I started turning the crank again, as bits of ice, splatters of fire, and showers of sparks fell around us.

"How are they shooting at us?" Lilahh panted.

"Probably took the shields down when they sounded the alarm. Lets them attack more easily. Just keep turning, it's almost enough to climb out."

"We can't climb out with those guards firing at us!"

At that moment there was a large explosion near the pier and the firing ceased.

"Now!" I yelled as I grabbed Jaydahh and hurled myself out of the opening and into the water. I turned over on my back, holding the unconscious troll against my chest and stroked for the dock. I noticed people running around on the aft deck of the ship, firing spells at us, but they all fizzled away before reaching us. Then a huge hand grabbed the back of my tunic and I and the troll were lifted bodily from the water and dumped on the dock. Lilahh and Rikk climbed up after us.

"Thanks, Sam," I gasped to the hulking figure over me.

"You are welcome, Betty, and it is a pleasure to see you, but we must go. Jewels's shield will be overwhelmed soon."

"Take her," I motioned at Jaydahh. "I'll get myself moving."

I pushed myself up and stumbled after Sam as he ran to a boathouse across the dock and several slips down from where the yacht was berthed. Lilahh ran at my side, partially holding me up and Rikk came after with Jewels floating along in the rear, focused on keeping her shield up. We ran into the boathouse, where a small vessel was tied up. Sam ran to open the waterside doors, and the rest of us climbed aboard. Lilah got the engines running while Jewels untied the mooring ropes. Sam leapt aboard and Lilah steered us out into open water, the sound of violence from the corporate yacht fading quickly.

"Now where?" I asked. "We need somewhere safe and nowhere in Banjall is that."

"Already planned out," Rikk answered. "But can you do something about my hands?"

He held out his hands, which were already swollen with burns.

"Rinse them in cold water and wrap them up," Lilahh shouted over the wind noise. "There's not much we can do but let them heal and try to keep them from getting infected."

I helped Jewels rummage around the boat until we found a med kit, which included a pain potion. Jewels chilled some water, we gave the potion to Rikk, then wrapped bandages around his hands. By the time we were finished, Lilah was steering us into a little cove. Sam jumped overboard and hauled the craft up onto the beach and we all clambered out.

"We've got three, maybe four days walking ahead of us," Rikk said. "She's going to have to walk with us. We can't carry her." He pointed at Jaydahh, now lying on the beach.

"Where are we going?" I asked.

"Oh, you'll love it," Rikk answered. "Nice, cozy little cottage in the woods. Very homey."

"You're kidding."

"Nope!" And Rikk cackled.

EIGHTEEN

Rikk's hut had not changed in the weeks since we left. Some of the foodstuffs we had left behind had to be taken out and thrown far away and the place left to air out, but it was only a little dusty and few spiders had yet taken up residence. We spent a day making the place livable for six people and then got down to work.

Jaydahh had been uncooperative on our trek through the woods and it took all our energy to keep her moving, along with shielding ourselves and foraging for food, so that we didn't even try to question her until we were settled in the hut. We sat Jaydahh on the floor and I sat, cross-legged, across from her.

"In the spirit of openness," I began, "I want to lay out what we want. Then you can help us figure out how you can, um, help us." Jaydahh snorted. I ignored her. "Here's the quick rundown. We know about the super juice you people feed your athletes. We also know someone is selling those potions to the public. We want that to stop. Questions?"

"Why were you polluting the supply?"

"We were trying to start a war between the corps and the clans."

"That was a pretty stupid plan."

"I think we've figured that out."

"So why come after me?"

I paused and looked around, "Why *did* you guys come after an exec? I thought you were just rescuing me."

Sam cleared his throat. "It was my idea, Betty. When the DQI yacht entered Banjall, I thought we could kidnap an executive from the yacht and trade for you. We did not know you were also on the yacht."

Jaydahh laughed. A long, drawn out guffaw. "You people are some of the most inept clowns I've ever had to deal with. Let me draw the picture, okay?" She took a deep breath to calm herself and continued.

"We at DQI categorically deny that any athletes on The Pirates use any enhancing potions at all."

"Now it's my turn to laugh. I've talked with the equipment manager of The Pirates and I know what's going down."

"*For the record*, DQI denies any involvement in 'juicing,' as I believe it is sometimes called. Off the record, we're just as upset about the potions leaking into the general populace as you are."

"What?"

"Shut up and listen to me, Mr. Sterling. Tricrosse is not a...profitable exercise; however, it has its uses in keeping the general population entertained and...distracted. We cannot afford for juicing to become not just 'a' story, but 'THE' story of the month. People tacitly acknowledge juicing is taking place, but ignore it in favor of cheering on their favorite team. As long as the athletes' habits do not leech out into the public square, this arrangement works.

"The dissemination of the athletes' potions to other parties was, as you can imagine, a public relations nightmare. As head of Customer Relations, I was tasked with tracking down the source of the leak and plugging it. I was...not successful. Whoever is doing this is smarter than I am." Jaydahh said the last with pain in her voice.

"Then the inert potions began showing up in the supply chain. This disrupted both our athletic training programs as well as disturbed the black market chain. You HAVE started a war, a war among addicts and their suppliers. The underground markets in Fisk are about to explode. We did track YOU down and came here to stop you and find out the extent of your network." The troll slowly scanned the other four. "Some 'network.'"

I ignored her slight. "What's happening in Fisk?"

"If you thought some people exploding in a bar was bad...Couriers are being killed for delivering fakes. Addicts are raiding alchemy shops. The psycasters are starting to ask hard questions and a couple have been snooping around the Tricrosse training facilities. This whole thing is going to blow into a huge scandal and heads will roll. And I don't mean figuratively."

"May I interrupt?" Sam interrupted. "Am I to understand that we—your corporation and our employer—want the same thing? To cease distribution of increased effect potions to the public?"

"Who's your employer?"

"Irrelevant," I snapped. "Is Sam right? Are you after the same thing we are?"

"DQI has a vested interest in preventing public harm from juicing, provided you are willing to leave our athletic regimens alone."

"So..." I said, "all of...this, was for nothing?"

The rest of my team just stared at the ground while Jaydahh stared at me. I chewed my moustache and finally said, "Untie her leg."

Lilahh reached over to untie the rope around Jaydahh's leg, but couldn't get her hands near it. "Jewels, release the shield."

"No. I don't trust this cat. Her story stinks like elf cheese. We need to probe her. I'll hold her mind open and you read it."

"Jewels! I would never probe anyone against their will."

"And that makes you weak. We need to know what's really happening out there. She's a neutral, it'll be easy."

Jaydahh laughed. "You people really are clowns. I've heard enough." She stood up. "Repeat anything I've said here and you'll be destroyed. Stop spiking the supply and let the corps handle this." She disappeared.

"What!" Jewels screamed. "How did she hide she was a tech from me? That dirty cat, I'm going to..."

"Jewels!" Sam's voice was forceful. "Let it be. We have to act and we have to act as quickly as possible."

"Why, Sam?" I was tired and it showed in my voice. "She's after the same thing we are. At this point, I think we're done. Like she said, let the corps handle it. The potions will get off the streets and that's that."

"No, Betty. I agree with Jewels. Her story does not ring true. As many resources as DQI has and with one of their top executives working on the problem, and they could not trace the illicit potions? No, we have to move and we have to move quickly. We are all surprised she is a transporter, but that is of no moment. She is already marshalling her forces. We must get back to Fisk as soon as we can if we want to find out what her next move is."

"Good luck with that, ogre," said Rikk. "It'll take us a week or more to get back to Fisk. She's already back at her boat, or maybe she blinked straight back to her corner office in Fisk. Doesn't matter. We're too far behind to follow her. We have to get ahead of her."

"And, how, pray tell, are we to do that?"

Rikk looked over at Lilahh. "It's time to make peace with our past. We've got to go home."

I looked back-and-forth between the two Durgahh. "Wait. How does going back to the Treoynn help us? Aren't they just going to kill us? Or worse?"

Rikk chuckled. "I'll ignore the 'worse' thing. The Treoynn make the potions. They'll take Lilahh, me, and the elf to help them make better potions. We'll make sure they leave you and the ogre alone. We attack this problem from the other end. We make Treoynn the best potion-makers and the corps will send their top buyers to compete for the business. We'll have an in directly to their supply chain."

"And then what?" I asked.

"If the Treoynn are making the best potions, who is going to bid the most to get exclusive access to those potions?"

I've said I'm dumb, but I'm not stupid. "The person who is behind the public distro system."

Rikk chuckled again, "We and the corps have spent all this time chasing around behind whoever-this-is, trying to hunt him down. We'll make him come to us."

"Or her," Jewels added viciously, staring at the now empty spot where Jaydahh had been.

NINETEEN

We stood several lengths outside the main gate of the Treoynn village. Runners had been sent to the chief, and we were waiting for the response. I decided to broach the potion-making subject again. Rikk hadn't wanted to listen to me and Lilahh was strangely silent. Jewels, of course, didn't care—even welcomed the opportunity.

"Look, I get the plan. Make great potions, get the buyer to come to us, take him down. OK, great. Good. What's NOT good is the "make potions" part. I've never juiced, never wanted to, but I ignored those who did. Now...now it makes me...uncomfortable that we're going to be involved in making potions."

"We've been over this, son." Rikk's patronizing tone set me on edge. "I was one of the best potion-makers in Durgaland during my time, and Lilahh's got my abilities—maybe even more so. I know the elf can hold her own, too. Nobody's gonna get hurt using our potions. That's why they'll be such huge demand."

"I'm not worried about the 'getting hurt' part, I'm worried about the 'using' part. I don't like that we're enabling these people..."

"Who are gonna be juicing no matter what," Rikk interrupted. "We're not makin' 'em juice, we're just using their habits to find the person who's really hurting them. Once we've got him, we stop and go back to our regular lives."

"You don't owe these people anything, Betty," Jewels contributed. "Besides, you used to mess people up all the time when you were a bull."

I winced, and then felt worse when I saw the hurt on Lilahh's face. "Thanks for the reminder, Jewels," I sulked, and walked away from the group.

Sam waited a few moments and then came over and sat next to me, which put his head roughly at the same height as mine. "You cannot escape your past, Betty."

"Doesn't mean I have to repeat it."

Sam was quiet, then turned to look as the Treoynn chief and several warriors came out of the village. They didn't look threatening, so he turned back to me.

"No, you cannot escape your past, but you can do better than your past. I agree with you that this whole situation is wrong, but I cannot put my finger on what might..." He trailed off and stared at the Treoynn now arguing with Rikk and Lilahh.

"We missed it," he breathed quietly. "It was right under our noses all this time and we missed it." The crowd of trolls looked over at us and then went back to their discussions.

"What are you talking about, Sam?" I kept my voice low as well.

Sam ticked his points off on his fingers. "Why did the Treoynn try to kill you? Why was DQI, with all its vast resources, unable to track down the potion ring in Fisk? Why would anyone within a corp risk the corporate public goodwill on what amounts, to the corps, as petty marks? Why did Lilahh's mother's clan not do more to help us? Why is that chief right now negotiating with us rather than running us off?"

I was tracking with him now. "It's the trolls. The Treoynn are behind all of this and that chief over there is probably the head of the whole operation..." We both stared at the group near the gate.

"What now?" I asked.

"We play along. For the moment. We will, after all, be right inside the organization. Where better to strike?"

"We don't have any other choice, do we?" I grunted as Rikk motioned us to come join them.

As with my previous visit, the trolls were all smiles and welcome. You would have thought they had never tried to kill me or imprison Lilahh. They had nothing in their village suitable for an ogre, so Sam was forced to bunk in a hastily-erected tent with a thrown-together heater. I sat with him rather than go into the dining hall and we silently ate what was brought out to us. I gave Sam half my serving as they didn't bring enough to be more than a snack for an ogre.

I tried to act casual, but my stomach was churning almost as much as my head. How deep did this go? Was the Treoynn chief the head of the operation? Or did he answer to someone back in Ilanerra? My thoughts flickered to my conversation with Eddie at the Triangle. He had clammed up and kicked me out. Was he involved in the operation? How high did this whole thing go?

The thought we might be taking on an upper-level exec or even owner of a corp made me just a bit nauseated. As we finished eating, I turned to Sam.

"We've got to get out of here. This tribe is too remote to be running everything across the Straights. We've got to get a look inside and I know just where to start prying open a crack."

"I agree with you, Betty, but the Treoynn are not likely to let us leave peacefully."

I sighed. "I know. I know. I'll think of something."

"And if you do not, I will," chuckled Sam.

I left him in his shelter and headed for the chief's

house where we would be housed. There was a grand party taking place in the main hall, but I was in no mood to celebrate. I slipped around the revelers and made my way to the room Rikk and I were sharing. It was some time before he stumbled in, and landed straight on his bed, where he quickly fell asleep. I grunted as I watched him; I didn't think I was going to be able to sleep with all the worry clanging around in my brain.

I must have dozed off, though, because I came awake with a start at the sound of the door opening. I was sitting partially upright in my bed, still fully dressed, and I instinctively drew out a wand. A faint sliver of light, almost a less-dark bit of darkness, grew around the doorframe and I could make out shadowy figures crowding into the opening.

No one had made a sound except for soft breathing, so I decided not to wait for closer introductions. I aimed the fireball high, hitting the ceiling above the door. The explosion rained sparks and bits of burning wood down on the pair of trolls, with drawn weapons, that were trying to sneak into our room. I rolled off the far side of the bed, rolled across the floor to Rikk's bed, reached up and dragged him down on top of me.

If the explosion and the cries from the Treoynn hadn't woken him, he was awake now and sputtering, "What...?"

I pushed him off me and answered him only with a string of appropriate language punctuated by a constant refrain of, "Stupid, stupid" as I peeked up over the bed. The trolls had fled, presumably to get reinforcements. I pulled myself up to my knees and screamed as I pounded the mattress. That didn't seem to help release the tension, so I stood up and threw another fireball at the door while screaming, "Enough!"

Rikk had gotten to his feet and was still staring at me, slack-jawed. "What's going on Betty?"

I turned and glared at him, then put my face about an inch away from his. "These trolls," Rikk flinched as I curled the word out of my mouth, "are deeply involved in the potion ring. They tried to kill me once. They're trying to kill me, and you, and the girls and Sam. And I. Have had. Enough." I bit off each of the last few words and he recoiled from me.

I pulled my other wand and dissolved a large section of the exterior wall and stalked out into the space between the longhouse and the outer wall. Turning right, I counted steps and then dissolved another section of wall, leading me into the room shared by Lilahh and Jewels. I saw two trolls struggling on one of the beds and I launched myself at the bigger, burlier one. He just managed to turn himself so my shoulder took him in the chest and he attacked my back, but his angle was wrong and he lacked enough force for his dagger to penetrate my mail.

We fell heavily to the floor, distracting his partner who was trying to smother Jewels in the bed linens. He loosened his hold long enough for her to burn her fist through the sheets and she fired an ice spike that grazed his jaw and sent him stumbling back with a shout. Rikk had followed me into the room and he climbed over a still-stunned Lilahh and tried to untangle Jewels, and the second troll fled.

The first troll and I were still wrestling on the floor. He was big and strong for a troll, but not quite as big and strong as me. I got a grip on his palm and twisted his arm until he flipped his body trying to ease the pain, and then I pushed up on his arm, driving his face down into the floor.

"Put him to sleep," I grunted between clenched teeth. Rikk swiftly knelt and removed the troll's dragon-hide cap and almost immediately he stopped struggling and his body went limp.

"Thanks," I said, looking up at Lilahh. She shook her head and pointed at Jewels. The elf was floating above the bed and her face was twisted into a mask of fury I had never before seen.

"Those dirty cats," she hissed. "Let's go get them, Betty."

"I'm mad too," I said, "but there's a whole village

and we've got to get to Sam."

At that moment there was a very loud roar and the building shook.

"I think Sam already knows," Jewels said, and she flitted out the hole in the wall before I could do more than shout her name.

"C'mon, boy," Rikk said. "They'll gather a whole troop and be back and we've got to get my girl out of here."

I looked at Lilahh, who was sitting up in bed, but still obviously in shock.

"Bring her," I barked at Rikk and then ran out of the building and toward Sam's tent.

I ran into the middle of a mess. The tent had collapsed, trapping Sam and several trolls inside. There were muffled screams and grunts from inside the cloth. Jewels was flitting around in the air, firing spells at a small group of warriors who were attempting to surround her. She was so angry, she kept firing directly at them, and her spells fizzled on their dragon-hide armor, which only made her angrier, and more likely to just try to shoot them directly.

I used my nature wand to open a pit in the ground directly in front of a troll who fell in head first. This attracted the attention of his squad mates, who turned their attention to me. I shot a fireball at the feet of two, and they danced back, beating at the flames that singed the dragon-hide leggings they wore.

I bull-rushed one of the other trolls, who struck at me with a sword. I turned and let it skitter down the mail on my arm and drove the opposite elbow into his midriff. He doubled over and I grabbed the heel of his sword arm hand and twisted. He yelped and dropped the sword. I drove my palm up into his chin, snapping his head back and knocking him to the ground unconscious. With my entry into the fray, Jewels had calmed down enough that she was aiming her spells at the trolls' feet, keeping them busy avoiding the flames and ice she was flinging.

I grabbed the sword on the ground and began hacking at the ropes holding the tent canvas down. I had chopped through about half the ropes when Sam finally could rip the cloth away. He was tangled up with about a half-dozen trolls, all of whom were, by this point, motionless. Shouting and movement at the other end of the village warned of additional warriors on their way.

"We've got to go now!" I shouted and ran for the outer wall, which I dissolved. I ran into the clearing outside the wall and turned to look. Sam had stumbled to his feet and was herding Rikk and Lilahh out after me. Behind him, Jewels floated backward, shooting fireball after fireball at the trolls trying to chase us.

"C'mon!" I yelled. "Into the woods. We can turn and make a stand there with the trees for protection!"

We all made it into the line of trees and collapsed behind the largest trunks we could find. The trolls did not immediately follow.

"Are they gonna let us go?" I panted.

"No," Rikk answered. "They're gearing up for a hunt. We won't outrun Durgahh hunters and I can't grow a tree around all of us."

"We're going to have to fight them here, then," I said.

"It is just you and Jewels," Sam said. "Rikk and Lilahh have little tech that would be useful offensively in this situation and I have no tech at all and no weapons."

"We can handle 'em," Jewels spat. "Just give me a chance. I'll show those cats a thing or two about tangling with an elf."

"Keep it under control, Jewels. You take Sam and circle around to the other side of the village. We can divide and conquer. Any that get through your spells, Sam can surely find a tree branch or..."

"Daddy!" Lilahh's strangled cry interrupted my speech and we all turned to look at her. She had a wild look in her eyes. She huddled up to her father and repeated herself.

"Daddy. Dragon." Before our eyes Lilahh had been reduced to almost a child-like state.

"What? Where?" Rikk asked.

"Close. It's hungry, Daddy."

"Jewels," I snapped.

The elf's eyes glazed over and she slowly sank to the ground as her effort at mind-reading dampened her levitation. Finally she pointed toward the rear of the village.

"It's over there. Somewhere. Not too far back into the trees. It's mad with hunger."

"How are you reading it, Jewels?" Sam queried. "The dragon's hide blocks all spells, does it not?"

"I'm not really reading it," Jewels answered. "I can't read any thoughts, but its emotions are so intense it's kind of like a mist around it. The main thing I'm getting right now is hunger. But there's all sorts of other stuff mixed up in there."

"Fascinating," Sam responded. "I wonder if there are applications where a tech could use this to sense the approach even of shielded..."

Sam and Jewels would chat about tech all night, and we didn't have all night. Without thinking too much about what I was going to do, I jumped out into the clearing and ran in the direction Jewels had pointed. Shouts from the village told me I had been seen. Good. The more trolls following me, the merrier.

As I ran, I became aware of a low, rumbling grunt from the trees ahead of me, and, then, there it was.

A large, dirty-gray dragon burst out of the trees ahead of me and to my left. It was probably my imagination, but it looked much bigger than the one I had tangled with on my first trip to the village. I stopped so suddenly I almost fell. The dragon was growling and its teeth were bared. I shot a fireball at its feet, which caused it to rear up and roar. So I shot it in the mouth.

The scream was horrific. I turned and ran. I was gratified to see a large group of warriors standing, shocked, directly in my path. But they were so far back I was pretty sure the dragon was going to get to me before I got to them. Then, suddenly, I was flying. I looked up and grinned at Jewels, who returned my grin with a twisted grimace. We flew over the gaping trolls, one of whom had just enough presence of mind to throw a spear at us, then the dragon barreled into them.

Jewels carried me into the trees where the other three waited. The screams and roars and other sounds washed over us as the trolls and the dragon struggled. Lilahh was sobbing, her face buried in Rikk's chest. Rikk's own cheeks were tear-stained.

He squeezed his eyes shut. "I know why you did that, Betty, but I can't thank you for it. Let's go."

"Yes. Let's go," I said. I was still mad. "We've got to get back to Fisk. There's someone I want to talk to."

TWENTY

Eddie sat, trussed up in a chair, still a little wide-eyed. Being kidnapped out of your own bed and dragged off to an ogre's house will do that to someone. Sam only had a couple of human-sized chairs in the room and Eddie was tied to one, so I dragged the other so I could sit close to him. Jewels was out of his sight, sitting up on Sam's dining room table, where Sam also sat in a chair his size. Lilahh and Rikk were huddled up on Sam's couch, almost lost among the cushions.

We were one tired, bedraggled group, but I was still full of adrenaline. I knew Jewels was just as mad as me, and that was the only thing keeping us going. I think if not for that the others would have quit. They were more than ready to, especially after the dragon incident. The two trolls had almost mutinied when we reached Fisk, and it took a lot of sweet-talking from Sam to get them to help us with Eddie. And I don't think Sam's heart was fully invested either.

None of that mattered. I was determined to get to the bottom of this. I was a little tired of being hunted. It was time to do some hunting of my own.

I started in on Eddie easy. Asking his name. What he did for a living. Stuff I already knew and he knew I already knew so he wouldn't try to lie. That would relax him and keep his mind open for Jewels to get in a wedge, so when he tried to clam up, she would already be reading his thoughts.

I kept at him for a good while, trying to get him to admit something, but he kept denying any involvement in the illegal potion ring. He freely admitted to helping athletes juice and managing the supply of super juice, but he would get obviously nervous about any other questions and gave non-committal answers. Finally, he fell over asleep and I looked at Jewels.

"I got everything, Betty." Jewels was strangely calm. "It's the cats. It's always the cats." Some of her calm slipped away as she glared at Lilahh and Rikk.

"Just tell me what's going on, Jewels."

She looked back at me. "That blinker we caught on the boat..."

"Jaydahh?"

"Yeah, her. She's like the aunt of the chief that tried to kill us."

I whipped my head around to Rikk, my eyes asking

the question.

"What are you looking at me for? I didn't know he had an aunt."

"You lived there most of your life! She had to have been born before you left, she was way older than twenty."

"I'm tellin' you, son, I don't remember the old chief having any daughter, or any other sons, for that matter. The current chief is the only son of an only..." Rikk's voice trailed away and he looked a little startled.

"What? Spit it out."

"Well, the current chief's father was the only child of the old chief's second wife. His first wife was banished for..." His cheeks reddened a bit, "...for...um...having a very friendly relationship with another clan chief. It almost started a war, but, for some reason, the other chief backed down when she was banished and the Treoynn chief decided not to go to war. Funny thing was, that other clan was the Burgahh..."

"She was pregnant," I finished. "That other chief backed down to protect the baby and so Jaydahh is related to both the Burgah chief and the Treoynn chief and is probably using both...for what?" I directed the question to Jewels.

"Hostile takeover," Jewels answered. Lilahh gasped.

Jewels continued, "She's got grand designs of weakening the corps and hoarding profits from her potion running. Then, when their stock is cheap, she steps in and buys it up. That way two cat clans control at least one, maybe more, corps in Ilanerra and start running things over here."

"Eddie knew all that?"

"Most of it. He was the main buyer of juice in Fisk—the cat always used low-ranked guys from other corps so nothing could be traced back to her. Eddie was real close to her, though, 'cause he was in charge of getting regular potions to replace the extra super juice."

"I'm confused. I thought they were taking the extra strength stuff from the athletes' supply?"

"No, that would have hurt the teams. She wanted the players to stay upright, but the teams didn't use super juice for everybody. So their normal orders were a mix of regular strength and extra strength. The cat had her clans make all super juice, and Eddie was in charge of buying regular juice for replacements for all the teams the cat was supplying. He wasn't distributing the super juice to the public, but he was the distributor of regular potions for four teams in Fisk."

I rubbed my temples. "This is making my head hurt. It sounds way too complex. How does any of this help Jaydahh take over corps?"

Lilahh stepped in. "I can answer that, Betty. She makes profit selling the extra strength potions on the black market. Then, she blows the lid on the super juice potion use by the teams and how that's being leaked to the public. That gets people to turn against the sport and cuts into the corps' profits. That drives down corp stock. With low-priced stocks and the corps out of cash, she buys up controlling stock."

"Getting put in charge of the investigation into the potion ring must have been a stroke of luck," Sam interjected.

"That's what Eddie thought," Jewels added. "He couldn't believe she was the one investigating herself. Of course the investigations went nowhere. When our dummy potions started showing up in the supply, it actually helped them by raising public awareness of the problems. Only, it was too soon. The cat didn't have enough money yet, and came north to shut us down and keep a lid on everything. If we had waited a few more months, she probably would have left us alone and let open war break out in the streets of Fisk."

I shook my head. "This Jaydahh is way ahead of everyone. Including us. So now what? She just keeps running her scam? We've got a witness, but we can't use his testimony because we illegally mind-read him.

And by this time she knows we escaped the Treoynn and will be watching for us. Not to mention she's a blinker and will always be able to just pop out whenever we get too close."

"Not all the time, Betty," Sam said.

"What?"

"Tricrosse games. The stadium is heavily shielded to prevent tech use by the fans. If she is in a corporate box in the stands, she will be vulnerable. But only to a direct, physical assault. And we'll have to carry him," he gestured to Eddie, "with us. We break into the box, force the executives to listen to us, and give them Eddie. They'll take him and Jaydahh and...deal with them on their own terms."

"That's the best we've got?"

"I am afraid so."

"And all the people who have died?' Lilahh's voice from the couch was small and strained.

Sam turned and looked at her in silence for a while, his face sad and tired. "The only justice for them is that no one else need suffer."

TWENTY-ONE

"I don't care, Sam, I'm out."

"We need you, Jewels."

"No. You. Don't. You know as well as I do I'm no use in a fight without tech, you big dummy."

"But you have come this far..."

"And that's it! I kind of find this all amusing. If this blinker cat gets her way, the corps will go to war with the cats and that's bad for the cats. Anything that's bad for them is good for me. If you go in there and stop her, it stops the war. I'd rather see the corps and cats bloody each other up a bit."

"That's not fair, Jewels," I said before Sam could respond. "You're actually cheering for people to be killed."

"Not 'people,' Betty, cats. Trolls. Or 'Duuurgaaah' if you want to be polite about it. Let 'em die."

"Jewels!"

"Give it a rest, Betty. I'm not looking for your

approval. You've already dragged me around that forsaken country and nearly got me killed. And for what? To help the cats?"

"To help everyone, Jewels," Sam said. "Many people—not just Durgahh, but elves, ogres, and humans—will die."

"All people who work for the corps or are dumb enough to juice."

"This is beneath you, Jewels," I said without thinking.

"Is that an elf joke, Betty? Huh?"

"No, Jewels, I..."

"Save it. Save the cats. Whatever. Just do it without me."

Sam and I just stared at each other for a while after Jewels left.

"Well?" I broke the silence.

"We know Jewels is prejudiced. We pushed her too far."

"Yeah, but as much as I like Lilahh and Rikk, Jewels is our best tech."

"But, she was right, Betty. Where we are planning to confront Jaydahh and her employers, tech will be useless."

"I know, but I don't like to be limited in any area, even if it's supposedly useless." I sighed. "OK, let's go over the plan again before we go pick up Lilahh and

Rikk. I'm just glad they weren't around to hear that."

"According to the information from Eddie, DQI, the company that employs Jaydahh, owns Box 42, which is on the fourth floor of the stadium. Tech is prohibited within the entire stadium with the exception of the field and the locker rooms. The locker rooms are not shielded to allow doctors to treat injuries, thus, Lilahh will be able to mind-control Eddie, who will take her and her father into the locker rooms. There they will find a place to hide and keep Eddie under control and guarded until one of us comes for them.

"You and I will have to buy tickets. Once inside the stadium, we locate Box 42 and either cajole or force our way inside. Once inside, we accuse Jaydahh of threatening DQI and other corporations and ask to bring Eddie up as a collaborative witness."

"And the execs will listen to us, why?"

"Our hope is the unrest in Fisk has them worried and they will welcome any news as to what is behind the problems."

"We're getting almost as complicated as the corps. Alright, Sam, let's go get Lilahh, Rikk, and Eddie. The game will probably have started by the time we get everyone to the Triangle."

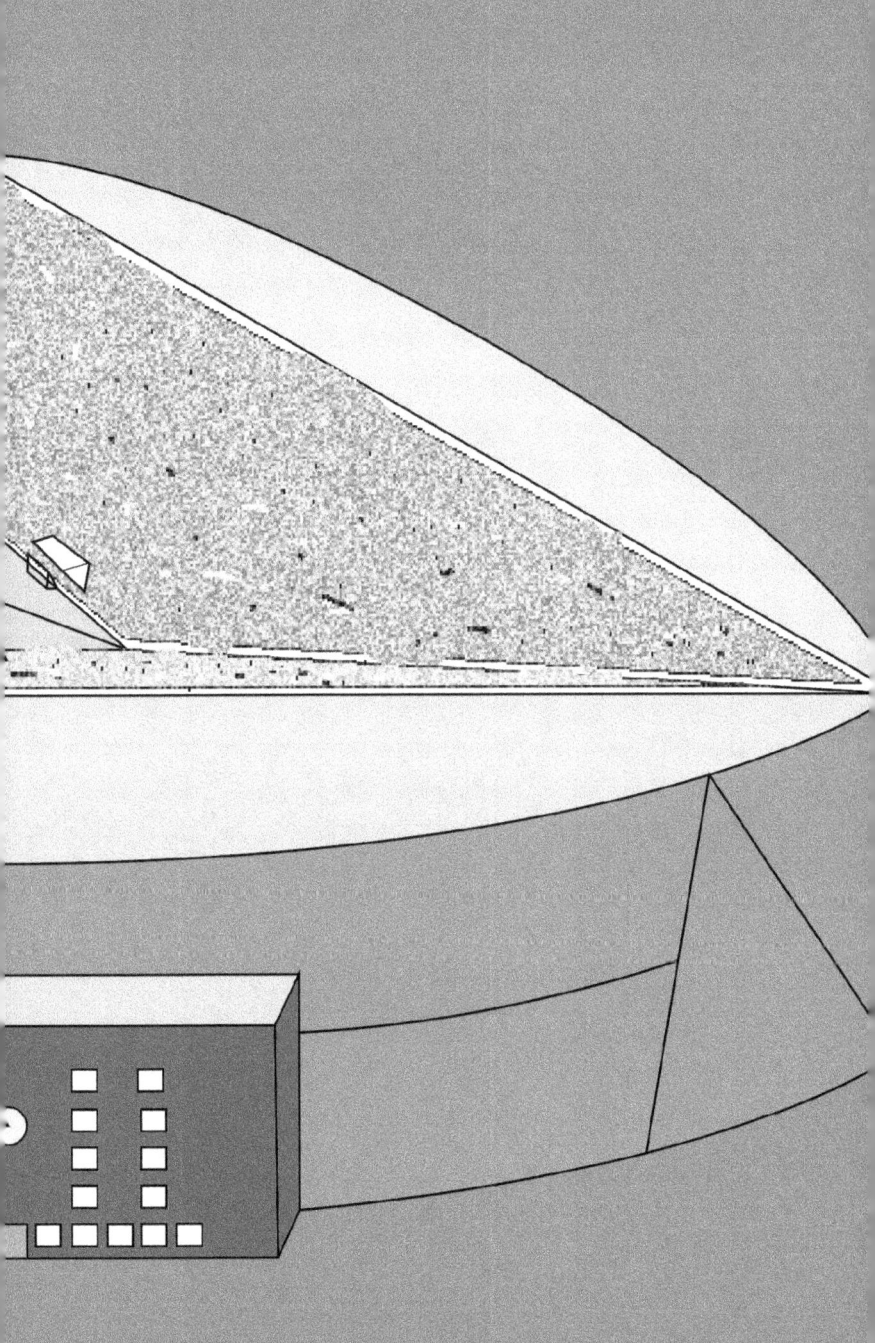

TWENTY-TWO

"I don't know how people can afford to come to these games," I said, staring at the tickets in my hand. "I hope Cristof can reimburse me for these."

Sam grunted. "You are lucky to have a benefactor. Most of the people here save all year for one outing, and many others are deeply in debt because they have purchased a package of tickets for the entire season."

I winced as I thought of what that must cost.

"This is how the corps maintain control. Focus people's attention and money where you want it and they will be compliant with everything else you arc doing. They will not have the money, and, thus, the independence, to do anything about those things they do not like."

"You sound like Cristof, Sam."

"From our brief meeting and what you have told me about him, I think he and I would get along quite well."

"And what about you, Sam? Are you compliant with the corps?"

"I am an independent, Betty. As are you, now, if you think about it. I do not need a corporate job, nor do you. And here we are, doing our little part to stop corporate machinations."

I sighed. "Do you think the others are inside by now?"

"I would think so," Sam answered. "When do you plan to go to Box 42?"

"Just after halftime. Jaydahh, if she suspects anything, will have relaxed by then. Not to mention the execs in the box, including her, will probably be a little tipsy."

"All the better, I suppose," said Sam. "We may as well watch the first half."

We climbed up through the stadium to our seats. I had bought the cheapest tickets available, which put us at the top of the tiers of seats and I couldn't really see anything. I had watched little Tricrosse in my life, which meant nothing made a lot of sense. Just tiny figures running around on the field, occasionally knocking one another down or scoring a goal. All of it accompanied by a great deal of cheering, swearing, and booing by the fans in the stands.

By halftime I was hot, tired, thirsty, and had a nasty headache. "I don't see what's so much fun about this," I grumbled as Sam and I shoved our way through the crowds in the cavernous hallways of the stadium.

"Everyone's tastes are different," Sam replied.

"Yeah, well, this is definitely not my taste," I snapped. "We need to get up to the fourth level. Where do you think Box 42 is located?"

"I do not know, but I am sure a security guard does," and Sam pointed at a uniformed ogre over near one of the entrance gates.

I hung back and let Sam approach the guard alone. The two ogres spoke for a moment and Sam headed back to me. "Box 42 is in the north section of the stadium. The guard said we can only enter the section if we have ID discs."

"Really? Let's go test that theory out." I strode into the crowd, then stopped. "Where's the north end of the stadium?"

Sam pointed the other way and we again pushed our way through the crowds, who were now trying to get back to their seats for the second half of the game. Sam stopped to talk to a couple more guards and finally led us to an information booth. A person there gave us a stadium map and we followed that to a stairwell close to Box 42 above us. We climbed up to the fourth level and found the way blocked. We needed ID just to get onto the fourth floor of the stadium, not to mention into any of the boxes. We slipped back down to the third floor.

"Brute force or guile?" I asked Sam.

"Are you any good at guile?"

"No," I admitted, "and neither are you. Brute force it is, then."

I bounded up the stairs. At the top, two ogres stood guard in front of double doors. I didn't bother to slow down, even as one of them started barking commands at me. I had spent my teenage years constantly forced to fight against ogres twice my size just to have the privilege of eating each day, so I went through the two of them without much trouble. There are several sensitive areas on an ogre's legs and if you know just where to strike, you can cripple them momentarily. I let Sam come up behind me knock them out and drag them inside. I might be able to fight an ogre, but I certainly can't move one.

The hall behind the doors wasn't empty. It wasn't anywhere near crowded like the lower levels, but there were still a good number of humans, plus some elves, trolls, and even a couple of ogres wandering the hallway. Most of them shouted or screamed and started running. One of the ogres ran toward me.

I ran at him and dove feet-first, sliding between his legs and pulling them out from under him. He pitched forward, landing hard on his hands. I rolled, jumped up and climbed onto his back. I punched hard at a spot where a human's kidney would be, but in an ogre was a nerve bundle just above his heart. He screamed and jerked spasmodically before passing out.

Sam had dragged the security guards into the hall and he and I rummaged around them to find any weapons. Sam came up with a couple of sais and I found a pair of nunchakus. They would have to do. There were already shouts coming from both directions in the hall. Sam and I sprinted in the direction of Box 42 and ran full-tilt into a mixed group of ogres and humans. The guards already had weapons of various types drawn, but they weren't prepared for two crazy people barreling into them.

I singled out a man with a staff and used the nunchakus to rip the staff from his hand. I preferred it to the batons anyway. I repaid his flimsy hold on the staff by flicking the tip up and breaking his nose before sweeping his legs and knocking him out. I rolled under a sai strike from an ogre and jabbed the end of my staff into his groin. I sprang to my feet and used my staff crosswise to shove two humans backward and got a slash from a sword for my inattention.

I whirled my staff and forced the swordsman and the other two humans to dance out of range. I felt a little trickle of wetness from my side and knew the sword had penetrated my mail, I just didn't know how much. I leapt toward the swordsman and engaged him in a series of strikes and ripostes. He was well-trained, but not against staffs, and I got through his guard with my extended reach. The tip of my staff caught him just below the eye and broke his cheekbone and he retreated.

I turned immediately to deal with the two I had let behind me and found Sam already dueling with them. I jabbed one in the kidney and he howled and dropped to his knees, so I let Sam deal with him and turned back to the swordsman. He had decided one blow was enough and was running away. I caught movement from the corner of my eye and threw myself down just in time to avoid a crushing blow from a staff wielded by an ogre.

The ogre's staff was nearly twice as long as mine and, if he had any training, he would probably beat me senseless. My only hope was to get inside his reach and engage him at close range. I dropped my staff and grabbed the nearest weapon, which was the sword recently abandoned by my opponent. I rolled swiftly to the right and again just avoided a blow from the ogre.

Yes, he was well-trained.

I kept rolling until I could get my feet under me and jump up. The staff was swinging around towards me again. This time I slapped it away with the sword and spun toward the ogre, bringing my sword around for a side cut. This also brought me in close to the ogre where he couldn't adequately use his staff to block my cut. I was taking a risk, if he was well-trained enough to step into me, I was probably toast because of the size difference.

He didn't. He tried to backpedal to use his superior reach instead of his superior size. This worked perfectly for me as I moved with him, threatening him with the point of the sword, which he kept trying to bat away. As he flailed about, he gave me an opening to slip under his staff and I stabbed him in the thigh. He yelled, dropped his staff, and fell backward and then scrambled away. I left him and turned back to Sam.

He was done with his...slightly more than...half of the guards. A door nearby was labeled "42 DQI." Sam tried the handle. It was locked.

"Kick it in?" I suggested.

Sam just glared at me.

"Alright. Quick, help me look, maybe one of these guys was assigned to this box and has a key." A brief period of searching turned up nothing.

Sam strode over to the door and knocked.

"Well, that was novel," I said.

He just shook his head. Very soon a voice called through the door, "Yes?"

"We mean you no harm. We need to talk about potions."

We heard nothing for what seemed an eternity,

then the door opened. The two of us were ushered into a well-appointed lounge with large windows overlooking the field. Around the remaining walls, large psycast panels displayed close-up images from the action still taking place below.

"How do those work?" I demanded.

"What?" asked one of the execs.

"There's no tech in the stadium. How are those panels working?"

The exec chuckled. "There's no tech in the stands or the lower floors. We have full tech in our boxes and on the field."

That's when I really looked around. Jaydahh wasn't there. If she had been, she had blinked out. I also noticed the wands aimed at us by several more security guards. I slumped into a chair. I began wishing Jewels had stuck with us.

The exec sank into a chair nearby. "Now, why don't you explain what this is about before we have you taken out."

Sam found appropriate seating and, between the two of us, we started relating the entire scheme for the exec. We hadn't got very far into the explanation before the exec sent most of the rest of the people out of the room and ordered Sam to take a security guard and go get the two Durgahh and Eddie.

Eddie, of course, started blubbering and denying

everything as soon as he was brought into the room. The exec kept at him, even though he was just repeating himself. I saw her glance over a time or two to someone sitting at the far side of the room, apparently very interested in a book. He nodded at one of her glances and I realized he had been mind-reading him. I looked over at Lilahh and she nodded to confirm my suspicion.

"That's enough, Mr...?"

"Markham, ma'am."

"Mr. Markham. Thank you for your help. You're fired."

"What?! But, ma'am, I done told you..."

"Quiet! Dharnash, take Mr. Markham down to his office and make sure he cleans out his personal effects only. Be sure to remove any corporate ID tokens he may possess. Inform security to have his psy-scans removed from our clearance system."

"Yes, Ms. Robertson," one of the larger ogre bodyguards said. He grabbed the still-sputtering Eddie by the shoulder and half-dragged, half-pushed him out the door. We all sat in silence for a while as the exec stared at us.

"Well. As for the rest of you...I think I'll send you two," she gestured to Rikk and Lilahh, "to the Treoynn as an appeasement gift."

"Appeasement?" I blurted out. "We just saved your

company from being taken over by them!"

"Yes, you did...what was your name again?"

"Sterling. Betty Sterling."

The exec chuckled. "Cute. You also disrupted our supply chains, nearly started a turf war in Fisk, and endangered our athletic programs. Not to mention incurred serious damage, injuries, and death in one of our supplier clans."

"So you're going to punish us for stopping the potion scams that were killing people here? What about Jaydahh?"

"We're punishing you for acting against the corps, even if our actions weren't in what you perceive to be the best interests of the public. Trust me, Mr. Sterling, we don't want the public at large to be hurt. A healthy, happy population is much better for our bottom line. As for our Ms. Burkahh, we'll probably promote her."

I couldn't speak, only gape at her. Lilahh gasped and Rikk shouted something unintelligible, or maybe it was troll.

Ms. Robertson shrugged her shoulders. "She's ambitious, smart, and has unique skills. She's been using that talent for her own aggrandizement. We'll move her up far enough that she will want to use her talent for us rather than herself. Now. I think, Mr. Sterling, you and your ogre friend will receive some time at a corp camp..."

I groaned. Corp camps were hard-labor prison camps. I had done a brief stint in one years ago when I failed to complete a job. The exec ignored my outburst and continued.

"...perhaps a year. Yes, I think that should be sufficient." She turned to the mind-reader. "Go with them to the security station in the basement and get their full identities and record their sentence in police records." She turned back to us. "These fine gentlemen," she waved around at the guards in the room, "will accompany you downstairs. Your troll friends will be packaged up for shipment to Durgaland, and you two will be processed for the Denton Mines Camp. Good day."

She turned her back on us and toward the large windows looking out on the field. I noticed the game was nearly over and the Pirates were comfortably ahead. This day, at lcast, DQI was winning everything.

TWENTY-THREE

The four of us shuffled out under the watchful wands of the guards.

"Don't go gettin' any ideas," one of them said. "We have an unshielded stairway down to the basement, so you'll be under wand the whole time."

I nodded glumly. I looked over at Rikk. "You'll take care of her, right?"

"I lost her once, boy, I'm not losing her again."

"Alright. Get out of here, then."

He nodded once and hugged Lilahh to himself. The guards were looking at us and at each other, not sure what we were talking about. Then the wooden floor under Rikk's feet dissolved and he and Lilah dropped into a throng of people milling around the concourse below. They immediately slipped into the crowd while the guards started yelling at each other and three dropped into the hole. The others had their wands out and pointed straight at Sam and me.

I raised my hands. "We've got no natural talent, guys. We'll go along peacefully."

Below us, yells and screams testified to the chaos the had been unleashed by armed security jumping into the crowd. The remaining guards marched Sam and me toward a stairway marked with "Corporate ID Only" signs. We were prodded down the stairs, but only made it down one floor before the chaos in the hall spilled into the stairwell.

Panicked people trying to escape the running throngs ignored the warning signs on the door and broke through and started trying to get down the stairs. The guards shouted and started trying to push their way through. I glanced at Sam and he raised his eyebrows and then we turned and raced back up the stairs.

We were up in the fourth floor hallway before there was any indication the guards had noticed our absence. We ran back toward the DQI suite, passing curious bystanders looking down through the hole in the floor and headed down the nearest stairs. As we headed down, we were pressed in by others. The whole stadium appeared to be in a rout by now. Sam might have normally stood out, but there were enough ogres in the crowd that we both blended in.

The crowds were so packed, no one could fall, which was fine because anyone falling would have been trampled. We squeezed and pushed and shoved our way down to the first floor and headed for an exit. Security at the gate might have stopped us, but any security guards had their hands full. We finally broke out into the floater lot and the crowds dispersed, until we spotted someone.

Sam and I both stopped and stared.

"Good afternoon, Betty! And you, Master Samhradh!" Cristof was beaming.

"How? Where?" I was totally befuddled.

"Walk with me, won't you?"

We fell in on either side of Cristof as he strode across the lot.

"As you know, Betty, I have a knack for keeping an eye on things, and I hire agents, such as yourself, to take care of things. I noticed you had cleaned up the problem with the potions, but were now in a bit of a bind yourself. I decided to come take a hand in pulling you out of your predicament. Mainly so I could talk to you for a bit.

"I'm...disappointed in the sheer amount of violence in your...solution to the problem. I'm not dismissing you, understand, but I would like you to work on finding more peaceful solutions to these little jobs I give you." He turned, "And that includes you, Samhradh. You're usually quite benign, but when you join up with Betty, your natural inclinations come a bit...unglued." Sam actually turned red. Not as red as me, but red.

"I suppose it could have been much worse," he continued. "Had Jewels been with you, there might have been a great deal more chaos. I can't say I agree with her attitude, but we'll take small victories where we can, no? But, enough about that. You both will be *persona non grata* in Fisk for some time, so I am going to send you on a little...let's call it a 'working vacation.'" He opened a package I had not noticed he was carrying. "Here is passage to Corin and details of the job." My eyes widened. "Yes, yes, I know the island is famous as a romantic getaway, but there's obviously none of that for you two.

"The passage by sea will take a week or so, and by the time you get there, do the job, and return, DQI will have quite given up trying to find you. I have a floater here so you can return to your apartments and pack. Have a wonderful trip!"

Cristof handed the package to me and walked off up the street, leaving us standing in front of a large floater with a chauffeur.

"Mr. Cristof!" I yelled after him. He turned. "What about Lilahh and Rikk?" I asked.

"We extracted your friends and are helping them relocate. You needn't worry!" He exclaimed cheerfully, and waved before turning and disappearing around the corner.

"Well?" I asked.

"I have always wanted to travel. I wonder if I can take my instruments?"

"I wonder what we need to do on an island paradise."

"Look at the job order."

I rifled through the contents of the package until I found a letter and skimmed through it. "He's sending us to help clean and repair stables."

"Seriously?"

I handed Sam the letter. He read it and sighed, then turned and looked at the screaming crowds still streaming out of the Triangle.

"I suppose, after all the mess we caused, cleaning up horse dung is poetic justice."

"Eh. It's better than a corp work camp." And we climbed in the floater.

THE END

Since 2005, Barry Scott Will has written 20 strategy guides for video games across a wide range of genres. His guides have sold several thousand copies and generated more than ten million hits on Web sites such as GameFAQs. His guides have received high praise from readers and won several awards. "The Long-Lost Troll" is his second novel set in a new type of fantasy world, one where using magic is as common as brushing your teeth. Barry currently resides in Virginia with his wife, three children, and ten video game systems.

Personal Web site: barryscottwill.com
Follow on Twitter: @PapaGamer
Like on Facebook: www.facebook.com/PapaGamer66

Read more about Betty Sterling's world at www.worldofberrea.com

Besides illustrations for *The Long-Lost Troll*, Ashton was the cover designer for *A Fine Basket of Fish* in 2013. His graphic designs are featured for the 2017-2018 season for the Lee-Davis Players. In 2016-2017, his artworks were exhibited in the Lee-Davis High School Art Show. A still life was displayed in the Hanover County Public Schools Superintendent's office. He has won nearly a dozen awards in the PTA Reflections contest through the years, most recently earning a state-level Award of Merit for Film Production in 2015. His art education began at the Virginia Museum of Fine Arts when he was 3 years old; more recently, Cheryl Dillard has been a key mentor. He has also taken a course at the Metropolitan Museum of Art. He plans to major in Communication Arts or Illustration with a focus on character design and graphic novelism.

On weekend evenings, Ashton hangs out with his friends in Advance College Academy—in person or via Twitch. He sings and dances in a show choir called Madz, does tech for the Lee-Davis Players and enjoys the Board Games Club.

Facebook SheepEtiquette or Ashton Will
Instagram @therealsheepetiquette
Twitter @SheepEtiquette